"I Want You To Wear My Engagement Ring."

Shock unfurled in Kate's toes. She didn't know what Duarte was up to. Right now he held all the cards.

"Seems to me like you have a fine sense of humor to suggest something as ridiculous as this. What do you really hope to accomplish?"

"If my father thinks I'm already locked into a relationship—" he skimmed his knuckles up her arm "—he will quit pressing me to marry one of his friends' daughters."

"Why choose me? Surely there must be plenty of women who would be quite happy to pretend to be your fiancée?"

"There are women who want to be my fiancée, but not pretend."

"What a shame you're suffering from such ego problems."

"I fully realize my bank balance offers a hefty enticer. With you, however, we both know where we stand."

Dear Reader,

Welcome to book 2 in my Rich, Rugged & Royal series about the mysterious Medina family!

What would you do if you crossed paths with a man who just happened to be a prince from a deposed royal family? And what if a photograph of that immensely hunky guy could be worth millions? How far would you go to snag that picture?

Photojournalist Kate Harper faces just that dilemma when she discovers the true identity of resort mogul Duarte Medina.

Duarte Medina is a man who will do anything to protect his family's privacy, and Kate Harper will stop at nothing to find out everything she can about the elusive Medina heir. In fact, the life of someone very dear to her depends on Kate's success in exposing the Medina secrets. All too soon, she finds herself unable to stop exposing her own heart to the dark and brooding royal!

Thank you for picking up Duarte and Kate's story. And don't miss the final installment of Rich, Rugged & Royal, *His Heir, Her Honor,* with Dr. Carlos Medina, in March.

Cheers!

Catherine Mann

www.catherinemann.com

CATHERINE MANN

HIS THIRTY-DAY FIANCÉE

Published by Silhouette Books
America's Publisher of Contemporary Romance

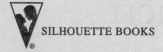 SILHOUETTE BOOKS

Recycling programs
for this product may
not exist in your area.

ISBN-13: 978-0-373-73074-2

HIS THIRTY-DAY FIANCÉE

Copyright © 2011 by Catherine Mann

Books by Catherine Mann

CATHERINE MANN

USA TODAY bestselling author Catherine Mann is living out her own fairy-tale ending on a sunny Florida beach with her Prince Charming husband and their four children. With more than thirty-five books in print in more than twenty countries, she has also celebrated wins for both a RITA® Award and a Booksellers' Best Award. Catherine enjoys chatting with readers online—thanks to the wonders of the wireless internet that allows her to network with her laptop by the water! To learn more about her work, visit her website, www.catherinemann.com, or reach her by snail mail at P.O. Box 6065, Navarre, FL 32566.

To Mollie Saunders,
a real-life princess and a magical storyteller!

One

Catching a royal was tough. But catching an elusive Medina was damn near impossible.

Teeth chattering, photojournalist Kate Harper inched along the third-story ledge leading to Prince Duarte Medina's living quarters. The planked exterior of his Martha's Vineyard resort offered precious little to grab hold of as she felt her way across in the dark, but she'd never been one to admit defeat.

Come hell or high water, she would snag her top-dollar picture. Her sister's future teetered even more precariously than Kate's balance on the twelve-inch beam.

Wind whipped in off the harbor, slapping her mossy green Dolce & Gabbana knockoff around her legs. Her cold toes curled along the wooden ridge since she'd ditched her heels on the balcony next door before climbing out. Thank God it wasn't snowing tonight.

Wrangling her way into an event at the posh Medina resort hadn't been easy. But she'd nabbed a ticket to a Fortune 500 mogul's rehearsal dinner for his son by promising a dimwit dilettante to run a tabloid piece on her ex in exchange for the woman's invitation. Once in, however, Kate was on her own to dodge security, locate Prince Duarte and snap the shot. As best she could tell, this was her only hope to enter his suite. Too bad her coat and gloves had been checked at the door.

The minicameras embedded in her earrings were about to tear her darn earlobes in half. She'd transformed a couple old button cameras into what looked like gold-and-emerald jewelry.

The lighthouse swooped a dim beam through the cottony-thick fog, Klaxon wailing every twenty seconds and temporarily drowning out the sound of wedding-party guests mingling on the first floor. She scooched closer to the prince's balcony.

Kate stretched her leg farther, farther still until… Pay dirt. Her pounding heart threatened to pop a seam on her thrift-shop satin gown. She grabbed the railing fast and swung her leg over.

A hand clamped around her wrist. A strong hand. A *masculine* hand.

She yelped as another hand grabbed her ankle and hauled, grip strong on her arm and calf. His fingers seared her freezing skin just over her anklet made by her sister. A good-luck charm to match the earrings. She sure hoped it helped.

A swift yank sent her tumbling over onto the balcony. Her dress twisted around her thighs and hopefully not higher. She scrambled for firm footing, her arms flailing as her gown slid back into place. She landed hard against a wall.

No, wait. Walls didn't have crisp chest hair and defined muscles, and smell of musky perspiration. Under normal circumstances, she'd have been more than a little turned on. If she wasn't so focused on her sister's future and her lips weren't turning blue from the cold.

Kate peeked…and found a broad male torso an inch from her nose. A black shirt or robe hung open, exposing darkly tanned skin and brown hair. Her fingers clenched in the silky fabric. Some kind of karate workout clothes?

Good God, did Medina actually hire ninjas for protection like monarchs in movies?

Kate looked up the strong column of the ninja's neck, the tensed line of his square jaw in need of a shave. Then, holy crap, she met the same coal-black eyes she'd been planning to photograph.

"You're not a ninja," she blurted.

"And you are not much of an acrobat." Prince Duarte Medina didn't smile, much less say cheese.

"Not since I flunked out of kinder-gym." This was the strangest conversation ever, but at least he hadn't pitched her over the railing. Yet.

He also didn't let go of her arms. The restrained strength of his calloused fingers sparked an unwelcomed shiver of awareness along her chilled skin.

Duarte glanced down at her bare feet. "Were you booted for a balance beam infraction?"

"Actually, I broke another kid's nose." She'd tripped the nasty little boy after he'd called her sister a moron.

Kate fingered her earring. She had to snap her pictures and punch out. This was an opportunity rarer than a red diamond.

The Medina monarchy had pretty much fallen off the map twenty-seven years ago after King Enrique Medina was deposed in a coup that left his wife dead. For decades rumors swirled that the old widower had walled up with his three sons in an Argentinean fortress. After a while, people stopped wondering about the Medinas at all. Until she'd felt the journalistic twitch to research an individual in the background of a photo she'd taken. That twitch had led to her news story which popped the top off a genie bottle. She'd exposed the secret lives of three now-grown princes who were hiding in plain sight in the United States.

But that hadn't been enough. The paycheck on that story hadn't come close to hauling her out of the financial difficulties life had thrust upon her.

Her window of opportunity to grab an up-close picture was shrinking. Already paparazzi from every corner of the globe were scrambling for a photo op now that news of her initial find leaked like water through a crumbling sandcastle.

Yet somehow, she'd beaten them all because Duarte Medina was really here. In the flesh. In front of her. And so much hotter in person. She swayed and couldn't even blame it on vertigo.

He scooped her into his arms, apparently sporting real strength to go with those ninja workout clothes.

"You are turning to a block of ice." His voice rumbled with the barest hint of an exotic accent, the bedroom sort of inflection perfect for voice-overs in commercials that would convince a woman to buy anything if he came with it. "You need to come in from the cold before you pass out."

So he could call security to lock her up? Her angle with the earring cameras wasn't great, but she hoped she'd snagged some workable shots while she jostled around in his arms.

"Uh, thanks for the save." Should she call him Prince Duarte or Your Majesty?

Coming into this, she'd envisioned getting her photos on the sly and hadn't thought to brush up on protocol when confronted with a prince in karate pajamas. A very hot, swarthy prince carrying her inside to his suite.

Now that she studied his face inches from hers, his ancestry was unmistakable. The Medina monarchy had originated on the small island of San Rinaldo off the coast of Spain. And in the charged moment she could see his bold Mediterranean heritage as clearly as his arrogance. With fog rolling along the rocky shore at his back through the open balcony doors, she could envision him reigning over his native land. In fact it was difficult to remember at all that he'd lived for so many years in the United States.

He set her on her feet again, her toes sinking for miles into the plush rug. The whole room spoke of understated wealth and power from the pristine white sofas, to the mahogany antique armoire, to a mammoth four-poster bed with posts as thick as tree trunks.

A bed? She tried to swallow. Her throat went dry.

Duarte smiled tightly, heavy lidded eyes assessing. "Ramon has really outdone himself this time."

"Ramon?" Her editor's name was Harold. "I'm not sure what you mean." But she would play along if it meant staying put a few minutes more. To get her pictures, of course.

"The father of the groom has a reputation for supplying the best, uh—" his pulse beat slowly along his bronzed neck "—companionship to woo his business associates, but you surpass them all in originality."

"Companionship?" Shock stunned her silent. He couldn't be implying what she thought.

"I assume he paid you well, given the whole elaborate entrance." His upper lip curled with a hint of disdain.

Paid companionship. Ah, hell. He thought she was a high-priced call girl. Or at least she hoped he thought high-priced. Well, she wasn't going that far for her sister, but maybe she could scavenge another angle for the story by sticking around just a question or two longer.

Kate placed a tentative hand on his shoulder. No way was she touching his bared chest. "How many times has he so generously gifted you?"

His smoky dark eyes streamed over the tops of her breasts darn near spilling out of the wretched thrift-store dress. "I have never availed myself of—how shall we say? Paid services."

A good journalist would ask. "Not even once?" Maybe she could inch just her pinky past his open neckline.

"Never." His hard tone left no room for doubt.

She held back her sigh of relief and let herself savor the heat of his skin under her touch.

Her fingers curled. "Oh, uh…just oh."

"I am a gentleman, after all. And as such, I can't simply send you back onto the balcony. Stay while I make arrangements to slip you out." His palm lay low on her waist. "Would you like a drink?"

Her stomach squeezed into an even tighter ball of anticipation. Why was she this hyped-up over an assignment? This was her job, one she was well-trained to do. Thoughts of her days as a photojournalist for news magazines bombarded her. Days when her assignments ranged from a Jerusalem pilgrimage to the aftermath of an earthquake in Indonesia.

Now, she worked for GlobalIntruder.com.

She stifled a hysterical laugh. God, what had she

sunk to? And what choice did she have with a shrinking newspaper industry?

Sure, she was nervous, damn it. This photo was about more than staying in the media game. It was about finding enough cash fast to make sure her special-needs sister wasn't booted out of her assisted-living facility next month. Jennifer had a grown-up's body with a child's mind. She needed protection and Kate was all she had left keeping her from becoming an adult ward of the state.

Too bad Kate was only a couple of rent payments away from bankruptcy court.

The prince's hand slid up her spine, clasping the back of her neck. Her traitorous body tingled.

She needed a moment to regroup—away from this guy's surprising allure—if she hoped to get the information she needed. "Is there a powder room nearby where I can freshen up while you pour the drinks? When I leave your suite, I shouldn't *look* like I climbed around outside the balcony."

"I'll show you the way."

Not what she had in mind. But she'd kept her cool during a mortar attack before. She could handle this. "Just point, please. I've got good internal navigational skills."

"I imagine you're good at a great many things." His breath heated over her neck as he dipped his head closer to speak. "I may have never had use for offers such as yours before, but I have to confess, there is something captivating about you."

Oh, boy.

His warm breath grazed her exposed shoulder, his lips so close to touching her skin without closing that final whisper for connection. Her breasts beaded against the already snug bodice of her gown. She pushed her heels deeper into the carpet to keep her balance. Her anklet rubbed against her other leg. Her good-luck charm from Jennifer. Remember her sister.

"About that bathroom?" Frantically, she looked around the bedroom suite with too many tall, paneled doors, all closed.

"Right over here." His words heated over her neck, raising goose bumps along her arms.

"Uh, but…" Was that breathy gasp hers? "I prefer to go solo."

"We wouldn't want you to get lost on your way." He stopped just at her earlobe as if to share a secret.

Had he touched her? His breath against her skin left her light-headed. He cupped the other side of her head. Hunger gnawed deep within her as she ached to lean into his cradling touch.

Then he backed away, his hand teasing a tempting trail and his black workout clothes rustling a lethal whisper. "Just through that door, Ms. Kate Harper."

Duarte gestured right, both of her earrings dangling from between his fingers.

Duarte had been waiting for this moment since the second he'd learned which tabloid scumbag had blown apart his family's carefully crafted privacy. He held Kate Harper's earrings in his hands along with her hopes of a new scoop. He'd been alerted she might be on the premises and determined her hidden cameras' locations before they'd left the balcony.

He'd spent his whole life dodging the press. He knew their tricks. His father had drummed into his sons at a young age how their safety depended on anonymity. They'd been protected, educated and, above all, trained.

Sweat trickled between his shoulder blades from his workout—a regimen that had been interrupted by security concerns.

One look at the intruder on the screen and he'd decided to see how far she would go.

In that form-fitting dress, she personified seduction. Like a pinup girl from days past, she had a timeless air and feminine allure that called to the primal male inside him. Good Lord, what a striking picture she would make draped on the white sofa just behind her. Or better yet, in his bed.

But he was an expert at self-control. And just calling to mind her two-bit profession made it easier to rein in his more instinctive thoughts.

Kate Harper perched a hand on her hip. "I can't believe you knew who I really was the whole time."

"From the second you left the party." He'd been sent pictures of her when he'd investigated the photojournalist who cracked a cover story that had survived intense scrutiny for decades.

Background photos of her portrayed something very different: an earthy woman in khaki pants and generic white T-shirts, no makeup, her sleek brown hair in an unpretentious ponytail as opposed to the windswept twist she wore now. A hint of cinnamon apple fragrance drifted his way.

Her bright red lips pursed tight with irritation. "Then why pretend I'm a call girl?"

"That's too high-class for the garbage you peddle." He pocketed her earrings, blocking thoughts of her pretty pout.

His family's life had been torn apart just when his father needed peace more than ever. Too much stress could kill Enrique Medina faster than any extremist assassin from San Rinaldo.

"So the gloves are off." She folded her arms over her chest, rubbing her hands along her skin. From fear or the cold ocean wind blasting through the open French doors? "What do you intend to do? Call your security or the police?"

"I have to admit, I wouldn't mind seeing more than gloves come off your deceitful body." Duarte closed the balcony doors with a click and a snick of a lock.

"Uh, listen, Prince Duarte, or Your Majesty, or whatever I'm supposed to call you." Her words tumbled faster and faster. "Let's both calm down."

He glanced over his shoulder, cocking an eyebrow.

"Okay, *I* will be calm. You be whatever you want." She swiped back a straggling hair with a shaky hand. "My point is I'm here. You don't want invasive media coverage. So why not pose for just one picture? It can be staged any way you choose. You can be in total control."

"Control? Is this some kind of game to you, like a child's video system where we pass the controller back and forth?" He stalked closer, his feet as bare as hers on the carpet. "Because for me, this isn't anywhere near a game. This is about my family's privacy, our safety."

Royals—even ones without a country—were never safe from threats. His mother had been killed in the rebellion overthrowing San Rinaldo, his older brother severely injured trying to save her. As a result, his father—King Enrique Medina—became obsessed with security. He'd constructed an impenetrable fortress on an island off the coast of St. Augustine, Florida, where he'd brought up his three young sons. Only when they'd become adults had Duarte and his brothers been able to break free. By scattering to the far corners of the U.S., they'd kept low profiles and were able to lead normal adult lives—with him on Martha's Vineyard, Antonio in Galveston Bay and Carlos in Tacoma.

Kate touched his wrist lightly. "I'm sorry about what has happened to your family, how you lost your mother."

Her touch seared at a raw spot hidden deep inside, prompting him to lash out in defense. Duarte sketched his knuckles over her bare ears. "How sorry are you?"

He had to give her credit. She didn't back down. She met his gaze dead-on with eyes bluer than the San Rinaldo waters he just barely remembered.

Kate pulled her hand away. "What about a picture of you in your ninja clothes lounging against the balcony railing?"

"How about a photo of you naked in my arms?"

She gasped. "Of all the arrogant, self-aggrandizing, pompous—"

"I'm a prince." He held up a finger. "But of course everyone knows that now, thanks to your top-notch journalistic instincts."

"You're angry. I get that." She inched behind the sofa as if putting a barrier between them, yet her spine stayed rigid, her eyes sparking icicles. "But just because you're royalty doesn't give you a free pass along with all these plush trappings."

He'd left his father's Florida fortress with nothing more than a suitcase full of clothes. Not that he intended to dole out that nugget for her next exposé. "Can't blame a prince for trying."

She didn't laugh. "Why did you let me in here? Am I simply around for your amusement so you can watch me flinch when you flush my camera?"

Kate Harper was a woman who regained her balance fast. He admired that. "You really want this picture."

Her fingers sunk so deep in the sofa that her short red nails disappeared. "More than you can possibly know."

How far would she go to get it?

For an immoral moment he considered testing those boundaries. His identity had been exposed already anyway, a reality that drained his father's waning strength. Anger singed the edges of his control, fueling memories of how soft Kate's skin had felt under his touch when he'd pulled her onto the balcony, how perfectly her curves had shaped themselves to his chest.

Turning away, he forced his more civilized nature to quench the heat. "You should leave now. Use the door directly behind you. The guard in the corridor will escort you out."

"You're not going to give me my camera back, are you?"

He pivoted toward her again. "No." He slid his hand in his pocket and toyed with her earrings. "Although, you're more than welcome to try to retrieve your jewelry."

"I prefer battles I have a chance of winning." Her lips tipped in a half smile. "Can I at least have a cigar to hock on eBay?"

Again she'd surprised him. He wasn't often entertained anymore. "You're funny. I like that."

"Give me my camera and I'll become a stand-up comedian—" she snapped her fingers "—that fast."

Who was this woman in an ill-fitting gown with an anklet made of silver yarn and white plastic beads? Most would have been nervous as hell or sucking up.

Although, perhaps she was smarter than the rest, in spite of her dubious profession.

This woman had cost him more than could be regained. He would forge ahead, but already his father feared for his sons' safety, a concern the ailing old man didn't need. An alarming possibility snaked through his mind, one he should have considered before. Damn the way she took the oxygen and reason from a room. What if her minicamera sent the photos instantly by remote to a portal? Photos already on their way to flood the media?

Photos of the two of them?

Duarte sifted the earrings between his fingers. A plan formed in his mind to safeguard against all possibilities, a way to satisfy his urges on every level—lust and revenge without any annoying loose ends. Some might think over such a large decision, but his father had taught him to trust his instincts.

"Ms. Harper," he said, closing in on her, following her behind the sofa. "I have another proposition instead."

"Uh, a *proposition?*" She stepped backed, bumping an end table, rattling the glass lamp filled with coins. "I thought we already cleared the air on that subject. Even I have limits."

"Too bad for both of us. That could have been…" He stopped mid-sentence and steadied the lamp—a gift from his brother Antonio—filled with Spanish doubloons from a shipwreck off San Rinaldo. No need to torment her for the hell of it, not when he had a more complex plan in mind. "It's not that kind of proposition. Believe me, I don't have to trade money—or media exclusives—for sex."

She eyed him warily, surreptitiously hitching up the

sinking neckline of her gown. "Then what kind of trade are we talking about here?"

He watched her every move. The way she picked at her painted thumbnail with her forefinger. How she rubbed her heel over the silly little anklet she wore. He savored up every bit of reeling her in, the plan growing more fulfilling by the second.

This was the best way. The only way. "I have a bit of a, uh, shall we say 'family situation.' My father is in ill health—as the world now knows thanks to your invasive investigative skills."

She winced visibly for the first time. "I'm very sorry about that. Truly." Then her nervousness fell away and her azure-blues gleamed with intelligence. "About the trade?"

"My father wants to see me settled down, married and ready to produce the next Medina heir. He even has a woman chosen—"

Her eyes went wide. "You have a fiancée?"

"My, how you reporters gobble up tidbits like fish snapping at crumbs on the water. But no. I do not have a fiancée." Irritation nipped, annoying him all the more since it signaled a bit of control sliding to her side. "If you want another bread crumb, don't anger me."

"My apologies again." She fingered her empty earlobe. "What about our trade?"

Back to the intriguing problem in front of him.

He would indulge those impulses with her later. When she was ready. And gauging by her air of desperation, it wouldn't take much persuasion. Just a little time he could buy while settling a score and easing his father's concerns about future heirs.

"As I said, my father is quite ill." Near death from the damage caused by hepatitis contracted during his days on the run. The doctors feared liver failure at any time. He shut off distracting images of his pale father. "Obviously I don't want to upset him while his health is so delicate."

"Of course not. Family is important." Her eyes filled with sympathy.

Ah. He'd found her weakness. The rest would be easy.

"Exactly. So, I have something you want, and you can give me something in return." He lifted her chilly hand and kissed her short red nails. Judging by the way her pupils dilated, this revenge would be a pleasure for them both. "You cost our family much with your photos, destroying our carefully crafted anonymity. Now, let's discuss how you're going to repay that debt."

Two

"Repay the debt," Kate repeated, certain he couldn't be implying what she'd thought. And she would look like a fool if she let him know what she'd assumed. She inched her chilly hand from his encompassing grip. "I'm going to work for you?"

"Nice try." He stepped closer, his ninja workout pants whispering a dark, sexy hello.

Holding her silence, she crossed her arms to hide her shivery response and keep him from moving closer. This man's magnetism was mighty inconvenient. Her toes curled into the Aubusson rug.

He tipped his head regally, drawing her attention to the strong column of his neck, his pulse steady and strong. "I want you to be my fiancée."

Shock unfurled her toes. "Are you smoking crack?"

"Never have. Never intend to." He clasped her wrists

and unfolded her arms slowly, deliberately until they stood closer still. His eyes bored into hers. "I'm stone-cold sober and completely serious. In case you haven't noticed, I do not joke."

Her breasts strained against the bodice of her dress with each breath growing deeper, more erratic. She didn't know what he was up to. Right now, he held all the cards, including all her photos.

Any hope of salvaging an article from this required playing with fire. "Seems to me like you have a fine sense of humor to suggest something as ridiculous as this. What do you really hope to accomplish?"

"If my father thinks I'm already locked into a relationship—" he skimmed his knuckles up her arm "—with you, he will quit pressing me to hook up with one of the daughters of his old pals from San Rinaldo."

"Why choose me?" She plucked his hand away with a nonchalance she certainly didn't feel inside. "Surely there must be plenty of women who would be quite happy to pretend to be your fiancée."

He leaned on the back of the sofa, muscular legs mouth-wateringly showcased in his ninja pants. "There are women who want to be my fiancée, but not pretend."

"What a shame you're suffering from such ego problems." She playfully kicked his bare foot with hers.

Oops. Wrong move. Her skin flamed from the simple touch. An answering heat sparked in his eyes.

It was just their feet, for pity's sake. Still, she'd never felt such an intense and instantaneous draw to a man in her life, and she resented her body's betrayal.

Heels staying on the ground, Duarte toed her anklet, flicking at the beads. "I fully realize my bank balance offers a hefty enticer. With you, however, we both know where we stand."

Her yarn and plastic contrasted sharply with his suite sporting exclusive artwork. The seascape paintings weren't from some roadside stand bought simply to accent a Martha's Vineyard decor. She recognized the distinctive brushstrokes of Spanish master painter Joaquín Sorolla y Bastida from her college art classes.

She forced herself not to twitch away from Duarte's power play, not too tough actually since the simple strokes felt so good against her adrenaline-pumped nerves. "Won't your father wonder why he's never heard you mention me before now?"

"We're not a Sunday-dinners sort of family. You can use that as a quote for articles if you wish, once we're finished."

Articles. Plural. But would they be timely enough to generate the money to settle her sister's bill for next month? "How long from now until that finish date?"

"My father has asked for thirty days of my time to handle estate business around the country while he's ill. You can accompany and compile notes for your exclusive. I'll be hitting a number of hot spots around the U.S., including a stop in Washington, D.C., for a black-tie dinner with some politicians who could put your name on the map. And of course you'll get to meet my family along the way. I ask only that I get to approve any material you plan to submit."

Thirty days?

She did a quick mental calculation of her finances and Jennifer's bills. With some pinching she could squeak through until then. Except what kind of scoop would she have when every news industry out there could have jumped in ahead of her? "The story could be cold by then. I need some assurance of a payoff—at work—that will help advance my career."

Bleck, but that made her sound money-grubbing. How come men struck hard bargains and they were corporate wizards, but the same standards didn't apply to women? She had a career to look after and responsibilities to her sister.

Duarte's eyes brimmed with cynicism. "So we're going to barter here? Quite bold on your part."

"Arrest me, then. I'll text a story from my jail cell. I'll describe the inside of your personal suite along with details about your aftershave and that birthmark right above your belly button. People can draw their own conclusions and believe me, the click-throughs will be plentiful."

"You're willing to insinuate we had an affair? You're prepared to compromise your journalistic integrity?"

For her sister? She didn't have any choice. "I work for the *Global Intruder.* Obviously journalistic integrity isn't a high priority."

A glint of respect flecked his eyes. "You drive a hard bargain. Good for you." He straightened, topping her by at least half a foot. "Let's get down to business, then. There's going to be a family wedding at the end of the month at my father's estate. If you hold up your end of the bargain for the next thirty days, you get exclusive photos of the private ceremony. The payoff from those photos should be more than adequate to meet your needs."

A Medina wedding? Wow. Just. Wow.

Before she could push a resounding yes past her lips, he continued, "And in a show of good faith, you can submit a short personal interview about our engagement."

"All I have to do is *pretend* to be your fiancée?" It sounded too good to be true. Could this Hail Mary pass for Jennifer work out just right?

"Of course it's pretend. I most certainly do not want you to be my real fiancée."

"You're serious here. You're actually going to take me with you to your father's estate?" And give her photos of a family wedding.

"Ah, I can see the dollar signs in your lovely eyes."

"Sure I want a story and I have bills to pay like anybody else—well, anybody other than Medinas—but I work for that payday." Hey wait, he thought her eyes were lovely? "What reporter in their right mind would say no to this? But what's the catch? Because I can't imagine anyone would willingly invite a reporter into the intimate circle of their lives. Especially someone with as many secrets as you."

"Let's call it a preemptive strike. Better to know the snake's identity rather than wonder. And I also gain four weeks of your charming presence."

Suddenly an ugly suspicion bloomed in her mind. "I'm not going to sleep with you to land this exclusive."

Her eyes darted back to the bed, an image blossoming in her brain of the two of them tangled together in the sheets, their discarded clothes mating on the floor in a silky blend of green and black.

A humorless chuckle rumbled in his chest. "You really are obsessed with having sex with me. First, you believe I've mistaken you for a prostitute. Then, you think I want to trade my story for time in your bed. Truly, I'm not that hard up."

She blinked away the dizzying fantasy he'd painted of the two of them together. "This just seems so... bizarre."

"My life is far from normal." The luxury that wrapped so effortlessly around him confirmed that.

"I should simply accept what you're offering at face value?"

"It's a month of your life to make appearances with a prince while I settle Dad's estate. Our family is rather well connected. You'll have some very influential new contacts for future stories."

Now, didn't he know how to tempt a girl? On too many levels. "If we're not sleeping together, what do you get out of this?"

He held up one finger, tapping it on her shoulder. "I give my father peace." He added a second touch, thumbing her collarbone. "I retain control of my own personal life. And three—" he curled his whole hand around her in a hold that was both arousing and a little dangerous "—I manage all cameras, all the time. You don't have access to any shots unless I okay them. The press hears nothing without my approval. And before you get too excited, when we go to my father's, you will not know where he lives."

She laughed in hopes of dispersing the tingles tightening her breasts. "Do you intend to put a bag over my head before you stuff me in a limo?"

"Nothing so plebian, my dear." His thumb continued to work its magic. "Suffice it to say, you will get on an airplane and then land on a private island, somewhere warmer than here in Massachusetts. Beyond that…" He shrugged, sliding past her, a hint of cedar drifting along with him.

Pivoting, she watched him stride across the room, his steps silent, his hips trim and decidedly hot. "You're taking me to an untraceable island so you can kill me and dump my body in the ocean for exposing your family—which, for the record, is just my job. Nothing personal."

Shaking his head, he stopped in front of a painting of a wooden sailboat beached on its side. "Pull a bag over your head? Feed you to the sharks? You are a bloodthirsty one." Pulling back the gold-framed artwork, he revealed a wall safe. Duarte punched in numbers and the door hissed open. "Nobody is going to kill anyone. We're going to let the world know we're engaged right away. Then if you disappear, all fingers will point to me."

"If they can find you on that 'warm island.'"

"Thanks to you, I'm sure my father's secluded hideaway will be found sooner or later." He pulled out one flat velvet box after another, each with an exclusive jeweler's name imprinted on the top. "One last point. If you break any of my rules about distribution of information, I will turn over the security footage of you breaking into my estate and press charges for unlawful entry. It won't matter that you've been my fiancée. The world will believe the tape was taken after our breakup and that you were a scorned woman bent on revenge."

The unrelenting line of his back, strong column of his neck exposed by closely shorn hair spoke of cool determination. She wasn't dealing with a rookie. "You would really send me to jail?"

"Only if you betray me. If you didn't want to play in the big leagues, then you shouldn't have climbed onto my balcony. You can always just walk away free and clear now." He plucked the smallest jewelry box from the back and creaked it open to reveal an emerald-cut ruby flanked with diamond baguettes. "Negotiations are over. Take it or leave it. That's my deal."

She eyed the platinum-set engagement ring, jewels

clearly perfect yet curiously understated. No gaudy Hollywood flash, but rather old-money class that appealed to her more than some princess-cut satellite dish in a six-pronged setting. For Jennifer's sake, she would make this work. She had to. She would regret it for the rest of her life if she didn't take this risk, a chance to provide for her sister forever.

Decision made, Kate extended her hand. "Why on earth would I betray you when we've obviously come to a mutually beneficial agreement?"

Duarte hardened his focus as he did in the workout room and plucked the ring out of the cushiony bed. Best not to think about any other kind of bed.

Cradling her left hand in his, he slid the ring in place, a ruby-and-diamond antique from the Medina family collection. He could buy her something more contemporary and ornate later, but now that he had Kate's agreement, he wasn't going to give her time to wriggle out. He had a month to exact revenge on her. And no, he wasn't going to dump her in the ocean or cause her any bodily harm.

Instead, he would seduce her completely, thoroughly and satisfyingly. He wanted this woman and would have pursued her regardless of how they'd crossed paths. But they hadn't met under normal circumstances. He couldn't forget what she'd done to his family. The best way to discredit any future reports from her would come from casting her in the role of a bitter ex.

A month should be plenty of time to accomplish all of his goals.

Closing his hand around hers, he sealed the ring in place. "The bride and groom have left the rehearsal dinner downstairs, so we will not be stealing their spotlight by showing up together."

"Together? Tonight?"

"Within the hour." He thumbed the ring until the ruby centered on top of her delicate finger. "I told you I wanted to spread the word soon."

"This is more than soon." She rubbed her foot against the yarn anklet, betraying nerves she didn't let show on her face.

"It's in your best interest that we establish ourselves as a couple right away." Just saying the word *couple* brought to mind images of how thoroughly he intended to couple with her. "Especially if you're still concerned about me feeding you to the fishes."

"Then, uh, okay. I guess there's no time like the present." She tugged up the bodice of her dress, drawing his eyes right back to her cleavage.

His teeth ached, he wanted her so much. He liked to think he appreciated the whole package when it came to women, mind as well as body. But good God, this woman had a chest that could send a strong man to his knees. He burned with the urge to ease down the sides of her gown and reveal each creamy swell, slowly taking his time to explore and appreciate with his hands, with his mouth.

Patience. "There's a large party downstairs with plenty of movers and shakers from social and political scenes. You'll get to share details with your boss. My word. Fifteen minutes downstairs and then I'll have the reassurance that you're committed. You'll have the reassurance that I can't kill you without pinging police radar."

"Okay, okay, I see your point." Her laughter tickled his ears. "It's just all moving so fast I want to make sure

I think of everything. I need to make one call before we go public."

"To your editor? I think not." He tugged her closer, the soft curves of her breasts grazing his chest. He could almost taste the milky softness of her skin. "I need your commitment to this plan first. Can't have you going rogue on me out there."

The fight crept back into her eyes, chasing away the nervousness he'd seen earlier. Her grit fired his insides every bit as much as her pinup-girl curves.

She locked his hand in a firm hold, her eyes meeting his dead-on. "I need to call my sister. We can put her on speakerphone if you don't trust me about what's being said, but I have to speak to her first. It's nonnegotiable. If the answer's no, then I'll accept your offer to walk away and settle for an exposé on your birthmark."

With the top of her head at nose level, he could smell the apple-fresh scent of her shampoo, see the rapid pulse in her neck bared by her upswept do. A simple slide of his hands around her back and he would be able to cup her bottom and cradle her between his legs before he kissed her. He couldn't remember when he'd wanted a woman this much. And although he tried to tell himself it had something to do with a stretch of abstinence since the Medina story broke, he knew full well he would have ached to have her anytime. Anywhere.

Why hadn't photos of her in the private investigator's report captured his attention the way she did now? He'd registered she was an attractive woman, but hadn't felt this gut-leveling kick. She chewed her bottom lip, and he realized he was staring.

His fingers tightened around her hand wearing his ring. "What about speaking to the rest of your family?"

"Just my sister," she said softly. Her eyes were wary but she didn't pull away. "What about *your* family?"

And would he tell his brothers the truth? He would have to decide on the best strategy for approaching them later. "They'll get the memo. You could call your sister immediately after we make our announcement downstairs."

She shook her head quickly, a light brown lock sliding loose to caress her cheek the way he longed to. "I don't want to risk any chance of her hearing it from someone else first." Kate tipped her chin defiantly, as if prepping for battle. "My sister is a special-needs adult. Okay? She will be confused if this leaks before I can speak to her. It's not like I would lie about something you can easily verify."

Every word she shared was so obviously against her will that his conscience engaged for the first time. But that couldn't change his course. Kate had set this in motion when she'd climbed onto the ledge, in fact back when she'd identified his face in a picture that launched an exposé on his family. Still, his inconvenient kick of conscience could be silenced by acquiescing to her request for a call.

"Fine, then." He unclipped his cell from his waistband and passed it to her. "Feel free to phone your sister before she finds out on Facebook. But I would hurry if I were you. We all know how quickly internet news can spread."

She scrunched her nose. "You cut me to the quick with your not-so-subtle reference to my news story of the century."

God, she was hot. And he wanted her.

While he would have to wait to have her, before the

night was over, he would claim a seal-the-deal kiss from his new fiancée.

Meanwhile, it wouldn't hurt to keep her on her toes. "Make your call quickly. You have until I've changed for our appearance downstairs."

With slow and unmistakably sexual deliberation, he untied the belt on his workout clothes.

Kate damn near swallowed her tongue. "Uh, do you want me to step into the hall?"

"You promised to use speakerphone, remember?" Duarte turned his back to her but he didn't leave. He simply strode toward the mahogany armoire.

The jacket slid from his shoulders.

Holy hell.

He draped the black silk over one of the open cabinet doors, muscles shifting along his back. She saw sparks like a camera flash snapping behind her retinas.

Oh. Right. She needed to breathe.

God, this man was ripped with long, lean—lethal— definition. She'd felt those muscles up close when she'd fallen against him on the balcony.

How much further would he carry this little display? Her fingers had been wowed, for sure, but her photographer eyes picked up everything she'd missed in that frantic moment earlier.

She was female. With a heartbeat. And swaying on her feet. The cell phone bit into her tight grip, reminding her of the reason she'd come here in the first place. Keeping Jennifer happy and secure was top priority.

Thumbing in her sister's number, she considered blowing off the whole speakerphone issue. But she'd probably pushed her luck far enough tonight. There was no reason not to let him hear and he would have

Jennifer's number anyway now that it was stored in his cell history.... And hey, might Jennifer have his as well after this call? Interesting. She would have to check once she could steal a moment away from him. She activated the speaker phone just as her sister picked up.

"Hello?" Jennifer's voice came through, hesitant, confused. "Who's this?"

"Jennifer? It's Katie, calling from a, uh, friend's phone." Her eyes zipped back to Duarte and his silky pants riding low on his trim hips. "I have some important news for you."

"Are you coming to see me?" She pictured Jennifer in her pj's, eating popcorn with other residents at the first-rate facility outside Boston.

"Not tonight, sweetie." She had a date with an honest-to-God prince. The absurdity of it all bubbled hysteria in her throat.

"Then when?"

That depended on a certain sexy stranger who was currently getting mouth-wateringly naked.

"I'm not sure, Jennifer, but I promise to try my best to make it as soon as possible."

Duarte pulled out a tuxedo and hung it on the door. She caught the reflection of his chest in the mirror inside the wardrobe. The expanse of chest she'd only seen a slice of from his open jacket—

"Katie?" Jennifer's voice cut through the airwaves. "What's your news?"

"Oh, uh...." She gulped in air for confidence—and to still her stuttering heart as Duarte knelt to select shoes. "I'm engaged."

"To be married?" Jennifer squealed. "When?"

Wincing, Kate opted to deliberately misunderstand

the whole timing question since there wasn't going to be a wedding. "He gave me a ring tonight."

"And you said yes." Her sister squealed again, her high-pitched excitement echoing around the room. "Who is he?"

At least she could answer the second question honestly. "He's someone I met through work. His name is Duarte."

"Duarte? That's a funny name. I've never heard it before. Do you think he would mind if I call him Artie? I like art class."

He glanced over his shoulder, an eyebrow arched, his first sign that he even noticed or cared that she was still in the room while he stripped.

Kate cradled the phone. "Artie is a nice name, but I think he prefers Duarte."

A quick smile chased across his face before he turned back to the tux. His thumbs hooked in the waistband of his whispery black workout pants. Oh, boy. Her breath went heavy in her lungs and she couldn't peel her eyes off him to save her soul. So silly. So wrong. And so compelling in his arrogant confidence.

Then she realized he was watching her watch him in the mirror. His eyes were dark and unreadable. But he wasn't laughing or mocking, because that would have shown, surely.

Silence stretched between them, his thumbs still hooked on the waistband. His biceps flexed in anticipation of motion.

She spun away, zeroing in on the conversation instead of the man. "You will probably see something in the paper, so I want you to understand. Duarte is a real-life Prince Charming."

God, it galled her to say that.

The whistle of sliding fabric carried, the squeak of the floor as he must have shuffled from foot to foot to step out of his pants.

"A Prince Charming? Like in the stories?" Jennifer gasped. "Cool. I can't wait to tell my friends."

What would all those friends think and say when they learned he was a prince in more than some fairy-tale fashion? Would people try to get to Duarte through especially vulnerable Jennifer? The increasing complications of what she'd committed to hit her. "Sweetie, please promise me that if people ask you any questions, you just tell them to ask your sister. Okay?"

Jennifer hesitated, background sounds of a television and bingo game bleeding through. "For how long?"

"I'll talk to you by tomorrow morning. I swear." And she always kept her promises to Jennifer. She always would.

"Okay, I promise, too. Not a word. Cross my heart. Love you, Katie."

"I love you, too, Jennifer. Forever and always."

The phone line went dead and Katie wondered if she'd done the right thing. Bottom line, she had to provide for her sister and right now her options were limited. The lure of those wedding photos tempted her. A family member, Duarte had said. One of his brothers? An unknown cousin? His father even?

A hanger clanked behind her and she resisted the urge to pivot back around. Right now she cursed her artistic imagination as it filled in the blanks. In her mind's eye, she could see those hard, long legs sliding into the fine fabric tailored to fit him. The zipper rasped and she decided it was safe to look.

Although that also put his chest back in her line of sight. He was facing her now, pulling his undershirt over his head, shoes on, his tuxedo pants a perfect fit as predicted. As the cotton cleared his face, his eyes were undiluted. And she could read him well now.

She saw desire.

Duarte was every bit as turned on as she was, which seemed ironic given she was wearing that god-awful dress and he was putting on a custom-cut tuxedo. Somewhere in that contrast, a compliment to her lurked if he could see past the thrift-store trappings of her unflattering dress.

"We need to talk about my sister," she blurted.

"Speak," he commanded.

Duarte carried this autocratic-prince thing a little far, but she wasn't in the mood to call him on it. She had other more pressing matters to address, making sure he fully understood about her sister.

"Earlier, I told you that my sister has special needs. I imagine you couldn't misunderstand after hearing our conversation." Hearing the childlike wordings with an adult pitch.

"I heard two sisters who are very close to each other," he said simply, striding toward the stack of jewelry boxes he'd set on a table beside the safe, his shirttails flapping. He creaked open the one on top to reveal shirt studs and cuff links, monogrammed, and no doubt platinum. "You said there's nobody else to call. What happened to the rest of your family?"

She watched his hands at work fastening his shirt and cuffs, struck again by the strange intimacy of watching a stranger dress. "Our mother died giving birth to Jennifer."

Glancing over at her, the first signs of some kind of genuine emotion flickered through his eyes. A hint of compassion turned his coal-dark eyes to more of a chocolate brown. "I am sorry to hear that."

The compassion lingered just for a second, but long enough to soften her stiff spine. "I wish I remembered more about her so I could tell Jennifer. I was seven when our mother died." Jennifer was twenty now. Kate had taken care of her since their father walked out once his youngest daughter turned eighteen. "We have a few photos and home videos of Mom."

"That is good." He nodded curtly, securing his cummerbund. "Did your mother's death have something to do with your sister's disability?"

She didn't like discussing this, and frankly considered it none of people's business, but if she would even consider being around this man for a full month, he needed to understand. Jennifer came first for her. "Our mother had an aneurysm during the delivery. The doctors delivered Jennifer as soon as possible, but she was deprived of oxygen for a long time. She's physically healthy, but suffered brain damage."

He looped his tie with an efficiency that could only come from frequent repetition. "How old is your sister?"

Now wasn't that a heartbreaking question? "She's an eight-year-old in a twenty-year-old's body."

"Where's your father?"

Sadly, not in hell yet. "He isn't in the picture."

"Not in the picture how?"

"As in, he's not a part of our lives now." Or ever again, if she had anything to say about contact with the self-centered jackass. Anger spiked through her so hot and furious she feared it might show in her eyes and reveal a major chink in her armor. "He skipped the country once

Jennifer turned eighteen. If you want to know more, hire a private investigator."

"You chose to be Jennifer's legal guardian." He slid his tuxedo coat off the hanger. "No law says you had to assume responsibility."

"Don't make it sound like she's a burden," she responded defensively. "She's my sister and I love her. Your family may not be close, but I am very close to Jennifer. If you do anything at all to hurt her, I will annihilate you in the press—"

"Hold on." He paused shrugging on his jacket. "No one said anything about hurting your sister. I will see to it that she's protected 24/7. Nobody will get near her."

How surprising that he would commit such resources to her family. She relaxed her guard partway, if not fully. She couldn't imagine ever being completely at ease around this man. "And you won't let your guards scare her?"

"They take into account the personality of whomever they're protecting. Your sister will be treated with sensitivity and professionalism."

"Thank you," she said softly, lacing her hands and resisting the urge to smooth his satiny lapels. She hadn't expected such quick and unreserved understanding from him.

"Turn around," he commanded softly, hypnotically, and without thinking she pivoted.

His hand grazed the back of her neck. Delicious awareness tingled along her skin. What was he doing? Hell, what was *she* doing?

Something chilly slithered over her heated skin, cold and metallic. Her fingers slid up to his fingers...

Jewels. Big ones. She gasped.

He cupped her shoulders and walked her toward the

full-length mirror inside the armoire door. "It's not bad for having to make do with what I had in the safe."

His eyes held hers as they had earlier when he'd been changing. Diamonds glinted around her neck in a platinum setting, enough jewels to take care of Jennifer for years.

"Stand still and I'll put on the matching earrings." They dangled from between his fingertips in much the same way her purloined camera earrings had earlier. Except these were worth a mint.

What if she lost one in a punch bowl?

"Can't I just have my own back?"

"I think not." He looped the earrings through effortlessly until a cascade of smaller diamonds shimmered from her ears almost to her shoulders. "I'll send a guard to retrieve your shoes, and then we can go."

"Go where?" she asked, her breath catching at his easy familiarity in dressing her. He sure knew his way around a woman's body.

Duarte offered his elbow. "Time to introduce my fiancée to the world."

Three

In a million years, he never would have guessed that tonight he would introduce a fiancée to Martha's Vineyard movers and shakers. Even though the engaged couple had left the rehearsal, the band, food and schmoozing would continue long into the night.

Duarte had expected to spend the bulk of his evening working out until he decided how to approach his father's request for a month of his time. He needed to simplify his life and instead he'd added a curvaceous complication.

No looking back, he reminded himself. And by introducing Kate to a ballroom full of people he ensured she couldn't fade away. Once in the Medina spotlight, always in the spotlight.

Kate stood at his side in the elevator—more private than the two flights of stairs. As the button for the ground level lit up, he slid his iPhone back into his pocket. He'd just sent a text to his head of security, ordering protection for Jennifer Harper, securing all the identification information for Kate. He would follow up on those instructions after the announcement.

The parting doors revealed the back hall, muffled sounds swelling inside. Clinking glasses and laughter mingled as guests downed crate after crate of Dom Perignon. A dance band finished a set and announced their break. His event planners oversaw these sorts of gigs, but he spot-checked details, especially for a seven-figure event.

Offering his arm to Kate, he gestured through the open elevator doors into the hall. This part of the resort was original to the hundred-year-old building, connecting to the newly constructed ballroom he'd added to accommodate larger events. He'd started his chain of resorts as a way to build a cash base of his own, independent of the Medina fortune.

While he spent most of his time in Martha's Vineyard, scooping up properties around the U.S. allowed him to move frequently, a key to staying undetected. There was no chain name for his acquisitions. Each establishment stood on its own as an exclusive getaway for hosting private events. He didn't have any interest in owning a home—his had been taken away long ago—so moving from hotel to hotel throughout the year posed no problem for him.

Kate's hand on his arm seared through his tuxedo, making him ache to feel her touch on his bare skin. His body was still on edge from the glide of her eyes on him as he changed.

Yet, listening to her on the phone with her sister, he'd been intrigued on a deeper level than just sex and revenge. Suddenly Kate's anklet of yarn and plastic beads made sense. There were layers to this woman that intrigued him, made him want her even more.

And he intended to make sure she wanted him every bit as much before he took her to bed.

Duarte stopped in front of the side door that would open into the ballroom reception area. He reached for the knob.

Her feet stumbled, ensconced in her retrieved black high heels. "You're really going to go through with this."

"The ring did not come out of a gum-ball machine."

"No kidding." She held it up, the light refracting off the ruby and diamonds. "Looks more like an heirloom, actually."

"It is, Katie."

"I'm Kate," she snapped. "Only Jennifer calls me Katie."

Jennifer, the sister who'd wanted to call him Artie. If his brothers heard, they would never let him live that one down.

"All right then, Kate, time to announce our arrival." He wondered what Kate thought of his other name, the one he'd called himself after leaving the island at eighteen. An assumed name he could no longer use thanks to her internet exposé. Now people would always think of him as Duarte Medina instead of Duarte Moreno, the name he'd assumed after leaving his father's island.

Sweeping the ballroom doors open, he scanned the tables and dance floor illuminated by crystal chandeliers, searching for the father of the groom. He spotted Ramon with his wife a few feet away.

The pharmaceutical heir smiled his welcome and

reached for the microphone. "Dear friends and family," he called for his guests' attention.

Some still milled over their dinner of beef tenderloin, stuffed with crab and scallops. Others collected around the stage waiting for the band to return from their break.

Ramon continued, "—please welcome our special guest who has generously graced us with his presence—"

Bowing and scraping was highly overrated.

"—Prince Duarte Medina."

Applause, gasps and the general crap he'd already grown weary of bounced around the half-toasted wedding guests who'd been whooping it up for a week's worth of celebration. Times like these he almost understood his father's decision to live in total seclusion.

Once the hubbub died down, Ramon pulled the mic to his mouth again. "A hearty welcome as well to his lovely date for the evening—"

Duarte stopped alongside Ramon and spoke, filling the room without artificial aid. "I hope you will all join me in celebrating a second happy event this evening. This lovely woman at my side, Kate Harper, has agreed to be my wife."

Lifting her left hand, he kissed her fingers, strategically displaying the ring. Cameras flashed, thanks to the select media that had been invited. Kate had been on target by calling her sister. This news would be all over the internet within the hour—just as he intended.

Comments jumbled on top of each other from the partyers, while Kate stayed silent, a smile pasted on her face. Smart woman. The less said, the better.

"Congratulations!"

"How did you two m—?"

"No wonder he dumped Chelsea—"

"Oh, you both must come to our—"

"Why haven't we heard anything about her before now?"

Duarte decided that last question deserved addressing. "Why would I let the press chew Kate alive before I could persuade her to marry me?"

Good-natured laughter increased, as did the curiosity in the sea of faces. He needed to divert their thoughts. And the best way?

Claim that kiss he'd been craving since the second he'd felt the give of Kate's soft body against him on the balcony.

Her ring hand still clasped in his, he folded her arm against his chest. The pulse in her wrist beat faster under his thumb, her pupils widening with a clear signal of awakening desire. She didn't like him, and he didn't like her much either after what she'd put his family through.

But neither of them could look away.

The whispers and shuffling from the guests dulled in his ears as he focused only on her. He brushed his mouth across hers, lightly, only close enough to graze the barest friction across her bottom lip. She gasped, opening just enough to send a surge of success through him. As much as he wanted to draw this out and see how long it would take her to melt fully against him, they did have an audience and this kiss served a purpose other than seduction.

Time to seal the deal.

A second after Duarte sealed his mouth to hers, Kate had to grab the front of his tuxedo jacket to keep from stumbling. Shock. It must be shock.

But her tingling body called her a great big liar.

The seductive rasp of his calloused hand cupping her face, the light tug on her bottom lip between his teeth threatened her balance far more than any surprise. Her fingers twisted tighter in the fine weave of fabric. Tingles sparked until her eyes fluttered closed, blocking out their audience, the very reason for this display in the first place. But whatever the reason, she wanted his mouth on hers.

Sure, the attraction had been evident from the start, but still she hadn't been prepared for this. There were kisses…

And then there were *kisses*.

Duarte's slow and deliberate intensity clearly qualified as one of the latter. Tension from the whole crazy night unfurled inside her, flooding her body with a roaring need that blocked out the gawkers and whispers. The cool firm pressure of his lips to hers—confident and persuasive—had her swaying against him, her clenched hands between them.

Memories of his bronzed flesh flashed through her mind. How much more of him would she see in the coming month? And if she was this tempted after a mere couple of hours together, how much worse might the attraction become with a month of these pretend fiancée kisses and touches?

His mandarin-cedar scent enfolded her as seductively as his arms. She splayed her fingers on the hard wall of his chest. The twitch of muscles under her touch offered a cold splash of reality.

What in the world was wrong with her that she could be so thoroughly entranced by a guy she'd just met? Her bank balance, her career, her sister's very future demanded she keep a level head.

Easier said than done when the stroke of his tongue along the seam of her lips sent a lightning bolt straight through her.

She pulled away sharply before she did something reckless, like ask him to continue this later. Kate scavenged a smile and gave Duarte a playful pat on the chest for the benefit of their witnesses, people dressed in designer clothes and wearing jewels that rivaled even those around her neck. This was his world, not hers. She was just a thirty-day guest and she would do well to remember that.

This party alone offered plenty of lavish reminders. Duarte took her arm and excused them both from the festivities. A legion of uniformed staff gathered the remains of the meal as she walked past. Her mouth watered at the leftover beef tenderloin, stuffed lobster tail…and wedding cake. Okay, technically it was a groom's cake for the rehearsal dinner, but still.

Her empty stomach grumbled. Embarrassed, she clapped a hand over it.

Lord, she loved wedding cake, had a serious weakness for it, which totally pissed her off since she considered herself far from a romantic. It was as if the cake called to her, laughing the whole time. *Mock me, will you?*

And speaking of negative vibes, more than one woman shot daggers with her eyes as Kate made her way back to the door with Duarte. She wanted to reassure them. She would be out of the picture soon. But somehow she didn't think that would help these females who'd set their hopes on a wealthy prince. One wafer-thin woman even dabbed at tears with a napkin.

Could that be the one somebody had said he'd dumped?

Arching up on her toes, Kate whispered against his chin, "Who's Chelsea?"

The question fell out of her mouth before she could think.

"Chelsea?" He glanced down. "Are you taking notes for the *Intruder* already?"

"Just curious." She shrugged more nonchalantly than she felt. "I am not a popular person among the young and eligible female crowd."

Duarte squeezed her hand on his elbow. "No one will dare be rude to you. They believe you're going to be a princess."

"For the next month anyway." With his kiss still singing on her lips, thirty days seemed like a very long time to resist him.

"I think we've milled around enough for now." He pushed through the side door back into the hall, deserted but for a security guard. The elevator doors stood open, at Duarte's beck and call as everyone else appeared to be around this place.

Once inside the private elevator, Kate stomped her foot. "What were you doing out there with that whole kiss?"

Duarte tapped his floor number. "They expected a kiss. We gave them a kiss."

"That wasn't a kiss." Her toes curled in her high-heeled pumps until the joints popped. "That was, well, a lot more than it needed to be to make your point."

His heated gaze swept down, his lashes longer than she'd noticed before. "How much more was it?"

The elevator cab shrunk in size, canned music suddenly romantic and mood setting. What a time to realize she'd never had sex in an elevator. Worse yet, what a time to realize she *wanted* to have sex in an elevator.

With Duarte.

She reached behind her neck to unhook the necklace. "Call me a cab so I can leave."

"How did you get here in the first place?" He caught the necklace that she all but threw at him to keep their hands from accidentally brushing. "Slow down before you tear off your earlobes."

"I came in a taxi." She slid the second cascade of diamonds from her earlobe. "I paid him to wait for an hour but that's long past, and I'm sure he's left."

"For the best, because really—" he extended his palm as she dropped the rest of the jewelry there "—do you think I trust you'll walk out of here and come back? We're past the point where you're free to punch out of our plan."

"I'll leave your damn ruby ring behind, too, and you can assign more of your guards to watch me." Would he threaten again to have her arrested? Would that really even hold up after the announcement they'd just made?

"That's not the point, and if you take off that engagement ring, you'll be losing the chance for those wedding photos."

The elevator doors swooshed open to his private quarters. He motioned for her to enter ahead of him. Going forward meant committing to the plan.

She stepped into the hall but no farther. Was this the point where he would turn into a jerk and proposition her? He had kissed her with skilled deliberation. "A part of our deal included no sex."

"I always keep my word. We will not have sex—unless you ask." He stepped closer. "Although be aware, there will be more kisses in the coming weeks. It's expected that I would shower my fiancée with affection. It's also expected that you would reciprocate."

"Fair enough," she conceded, then rushed to add, "but only when we're in public."

"That's logical. Know, too, though, that we will have to spend time alone with each other. This evening, for example, we need to get our stories straight before we face the world on a larger scale."

So much for her assumption of darker motives for his refusal to call a cab. What he said made sense. "Know that I'm staying under duress."

"Duly noted. Just keep remembering that black-tie dinner in D.C. with politicians and ambassadors."

"You're wicked bad with the temptation."

He steamed her with another smoky once-over. "You're one to lecture on that subject."

"I thought we were going to talk."

"We will. Soon." He stepped away and she exhaled. Hard. "I have a quick errand to take care of, but I'll have dinner sent up to your room while you wait. I hear tonight's special is tenderloin and stuffed lobster."

"And cake," she demanded, even knowing it wouldn't come close to satisfying the hunger gnawing as her insides tonight. "I really need a slice of that groom's cake."

Duarte watched his head of security shovel a bite of chocolate cake in his mouth in between reviewing surveillance footage and internet headlines on the multiple screens. A workaholic, Javier Cortez frequently ate on the job, rather than take off so much as a half hour for a meal. He even kept an extra suit in his office for days he didn't make it home.

Wheeling out a chair from the monitor station, Duarte

took a seat. "What were you able to pull together on security for Jennifer Harper?"

Javier swiped a napkin across his mouth before draping the white linen over his knee again. "Two members of our team are currently en route to her assisted-living facility outside Boston. They're already in phone contact with security there and will be reporting back to me within the hour."

"Excellent work, as always." He didn't dispense praise lightly, but Javier deserved it.

The head of security had also endured a crappy month every bit as bad as Duarte's. Javier's cousin, Alys, had betrayed the Medina family by confirming the *Global Intruder*'s suspicions about Duarte's identity. She had served as the inside source for other leaks as well, even offering up Enrique Medina's "love child" he'd fathered shortly after arriving in the U.S.

Javier had weathered intense scrutiny after Alys's betrayal had been discovered. He'd turned in his resignation the second his cousin had been confronted, vowing he bore no ill will against the Medinas and was shamed by his cousin's behavior.

Duarte had torn up the resignation. He trusted his instincts on this one.

How odd that he found it easier to trust Javier than his own father. That could have something to do with Enrique Medina's "love child" the whole world now knew about. Their grief-stricken widower father hadn't taken long to hook up with another woman. The affair had only lasted long enough to produce Eloisa. Duarte made a point of not blaming his half sister. He tried not to judge his father, but that part was tougher.

Making peace with the old man was more pressing than ever with Enrique's failing health.

Javier set aside his plate with a clink of the fork. "No disrespect, my friend, but are you sure you know what you're doing?"

Most wouldn't risk asking him such a personal question, but Javier's past wasn't that different from Duarte's. Javier's family had escaped San Rinaldo along with the king. Enrique had set up a compound in Argentina as a red herring. The press had believed the deposed king and his family had settled there.

However, the highly secured estate in South America had housed the close circle who'd been forced out of San Rinaldo with the Medinas—including the Reyes de la Cortez family. Javier understood fully the importance of security as well as the burning need to break free of smothering seclusion.

Duarte tapped a screen displaying an image of Kate at the antique dinner cart, plucking the long-stem red rose from the bud vase. "I know exactly what I was doing. I was introducing my fiancée to the world."

"Oh, really?" Javier leaned closer, pulling his tie from over his shoulder, where he must have draped it when he started his dinner. "Less than two hours ago she was scaling the side of the building to get a photo of you."

His eyes cruised back to the screen. Kate stroked the rose under her nose as she settled in the chair. Her brown hair tousled, her feet bare, she had the look of a woman who'd been thoroughly kissed and seduced.

Thinking of the way she'd made her entrance on the balcony earlier... He couldn't help but smile at her audacity. "Quite an entrance she makes."

"Now you've invited her into your inner sanctum?" Javier shook his head. "Why not simply hand over a journal with your life story?"

"What better way to watch your enemy than keeping

her close?" In his room. Where she waited for him now, savoring the beef tenderloin with the gusto of a woman who appreciated pleasures of the senses. "She will only see what I want her to see. The world will only know what I want it to know."

"And if she goes to the press later with the whole fake engagement?" Javier's eyes followed his to the screen, to Kate.

Duarte clicked off the image and the monitor went blank. "By then, people will label anything she says as the ramblings of a scorned woman. And if a handful of people believe her, what does that matter to me?"

"You really don't care." Javier tapped the now-dark screen, a skeptical look on his face.

"She will have served her purpose."

"You're a cold one."

"And you are not very deferential to the man who signs your extremely generous paychecks," he retorted, not at all irritated since he knew his friend was right. And a man needed people like that in his inner circle, individuals unafraid to declare when the emperor wore no clothes. "I assume you want to continue working for me?"

"You keep me on because I don't kowtow to you." Javier picked up his cake plate again. "You've never thought much of brownnosers. Perhaps that's why she intrigues you."

"I told you already—"

"Yeah, yeah, inner sanctum, blah-blah-blah." He shoveled a bite of the chocolate rum cake, smearing basket-weave frosting into the fork tines.

"Perhaps I am not as cold as you say. Revenge is sweet." So why wasn't he seeking this sort of "revenge" with Javier's cousin? Alys was attractive. They'd even dated briefly in the past.

"If you wanted revenge you could have gotten Kate Harper fired or arrested. She's snagged your interest."

Javier was too astute, part of what made him excel at his job as head of security. But then what was wrong with sleeping with Kate? In fact, an affair made perfect sense, lending credibility to their engagement.

"Kate is…entertaining. I'll grant her that." And his life was so damn boring of late.

Work did not provide a challenge. How many millions did a man need to make? He was a warrior without an army.

If he'd grown up in San Rinaldo, he would have served in her military. But with his history, he'd never had the option of signing on for service in his new home.

How ironic to be a thirty-five-year-old billionaire suffering from a career crisis? "She's also helping take heat off me with my father. The old man is in a frenzy to ensure the next generation of Medinas before he dies."

"Whatever you say, my friend." Javier tipped back a bottled water.

Ah, hell. He couldn't hide the truth from himself any more than from his friend. Duarte was off balance, tied up in knots over his father because he'd promised his mother he would watch Enrique's back. But how did a person defend someone against a failing liver?

He sometimes wondered why Beatriz had asked him when Carlos had been older, when Carlos had been the one to come through for her. She'd reminded him then he had always been the family's little soldier. He'd done his best to protect his family, a drive he saw equaled in Kate's eyes when she spoke of her sister. How ironic that their similar goals of protecting family put them so at odds.

Standing, Duarte returned the rolling chair under the console of monitors and tapped the blank screen that had held an image of Kate relishing her dinner. "Make sure you leave that one off. I'll take care of security in Kate's suite."

Four

Thank goodness no one was looking, because she'd tossed out table manners halfway through the lobster tail. Kate washed down the bite of chocolate rum cake with sparkling water. She was hungrier than she'd realized, having skipped supper due to nerves over crashing the Medina party.

Sipping from her crystal goblet, she opted for the Fuiggi water rather than the red wine. She needed to keep her mind clear around Duarte, especially after that kiss.

A promise of temporary pleasures that could lead to a host of regrets.

Footsteps sounded in the hall, a near-silent tread she was beginning to recognize as his. Would he go to his suite or stop by her room? He'd said he wanted to talk through details about their supposed dating past before they faced the world.

He stopped outside her door. Her toes curled. She licked her fork clean quickly and pushed away from the small table. Her shoes? Where had she ditched them before digging into her meal?

The door swung open.

Time had run out so she stayed seated, tucking her bare feet underneath the chair. Duarte filled the open frame to her room, blocking out the world behind him, reminding her that they were completely alone with each other and the memory of one unforgettable kiss. She straightened with as much nonchalance as she could, given her heart pumped as fast as a rapid-shot camera.

"Supper is to your liking?" He draped his tuxedo coat over the back of a carved mahogany chair.

"It's amazing and you know it." She wished she could take a slice of the cake to Jennifer.

"You were hungry." He loosened his tie.

Her heart stuttered. "How about you keep your pants on this time, cowboy."

"Whatever makes you happy, my dear."

Smiling, he slid the tie from his collar slowly, a sleigh bed with a fluffy comforter warm and inviting behind him. Then he stopped across from her at the intimate table for two, complete with silver and roses. Thank heaven he was still clothed—for the most part.

She placed her fork precisely along the top of her dessert china, the gold-rimmed pattern gleaming in the candlelight. "My compliments to your chef."

"I'll let him know." He scooped up her cut crystal glass of untasted wine and swirled the red vintage along the sides. "I have to confess, it's refreshing to hear a woman admit to appreciating a full dinner rather than models who starve themselves." He eyed her over the top of the Waterford goblet. "Eating can be a sensual experience."

Just the way he lingered over the word *sensual* with the slightest hint of an exotic accent made her mouth go moist. She swallowed hard and reminded herself to gather as much information as possible for future articles. While her primary job focused on taking the photos, an inside scoop could only help sell those shots.

This time with Duarte wasn't about her. She was here for her job, for her sister. "You don't strike me as the sort to overindulge when the dinner bell clangs. You seem very self-disciplined."

"How so?" He tipped back the glass.

She watched his throat work with a long swallow, his every move precise. "I would peg you as a health-food nut, a workout fiend."

"Do you have a problem with a sweaty round in the gym?"

"I don't love it, but I adore food more than I dislike exercise. So I log a few miles on a stationary bike when I can." Wait, how had this suddenly become about her when she was determined to learn more about him?

"You need to stay in shape for scaling ledges." He tapped the rim of his glass to her water goblet, right over the spot where her mouth had rested.

The *ting* of crystal against crystal resonated through her. "You said you saw me on security footage before I ever entered your room. What if those tapes of me crawling around outside somehow leak to the media? Won't that shoot a hole in our engagement story? And what about the part I played in exposing your half sister?"

"About the balcony incident, we'll blame it on the

paparazzi chasing you out of your room. As for Alys, we can always say you let it slip at work." He dropped into the chair across from her, lean and long, his power harnessed but humming.

"What's to stop me from claiming any of that if you decide to use the video feed against me?"

"Do you think I've revealed all the ammunition in my arsenal?" He turned the glass on the table, the thin stem so fragile in his hand.

"Are you trying to worry me?" She refused to be intimidated.

His breathing stayed even, but his eyes narrowed. "Only letting you know I play at an entirely different level than anyone you've ever come up against. I have to. The stakes are higher."

"I don't know about that." An image of Jennifer's smile when she'd passed over the braided anklet filled Kate's mind. "My stakes feel pretty high to me."

He set aside his drink and reached back into his tux jacket. His hand came back with a computer disc in a case. He slid it across the table toward her. "Copies of the photos from your camera and from my own press team for you to share with the *Intruder*."

"All of my photos?" she asked with surprise—and skepticism.

"Most of your photos." The hard angles of his face creased into a half smile. "You can pass these along to your editor. If he questions why you're still speaking to him when you have a rich fiancé, tell him that we want to control the release of information and as long as he plays nice, the flow will continue. I'll have a laptop computer sent up for you. I keep my word."

She traced an intricate *M* scrolled on a label, the

gilded letter taking on the shape of a crown. Her brain spun headlines… Medina Men. Medina Monarchs.

Medina Money, because without question pure gold rested under her fingertips. And he'd promised her so much more in four weeks. "I need to stop by my apartment tomorrow before we leave."

"Cat or dog?"

"What?" She glanced up quickly.

"Do you have a cat or a dog? What kind?" He cradled his iPhone in his broad palm. "I'll pass along the details to my assistant and your animal will be boarded."

His arrogance almost managed to overshadow his thoughtfulness. Almost, but not quite. "I didn't know that ninjas read minds. And it's a cat. I'm away from home too much to have a dog. My neighbor usually watches him for me."

"No need to bother your neighbor. My people will see to everything, like with your sister's security." He began tapping in instructions.

How easy it would be to let him take charge, especially when what he offered was actually helpful…even thoughtful. "That's nice of you. Thanks."

He waved aside her gratitude and continued texting. "Before you mention packing clothes, forget it. I'm already ordering everything you'll need. You'll have some of the new wardrobe by morning."

She glanced down at her green Gabbana knockoff. "Cinderella makeover time?"

"Believe me, you don't need a makeover. Even wearing a, uh—" He stumbled over his words for the first time, his brow furrowing.…

"A secondhand-store bargain, you mean?" She found his hesitation, this first sign of human emotion, unsettling…and a little charming. "You don't have to worry about offending me. I'm not embarrassed by the fact my bank balance is smaller than yours. That's just a fact."

"Very good that you're not going to waste our time with ridiculous arguments. What's your dress size?"

"Eight for dresses, pants, shirts."

"Got it." He input the information. "Shoe size."

"Seven. Narrow."

"Bra?"

She gasped. "Excuse me?"

"What is your bra size?" He quirked an eyebrow, without raising his onyx gaze. "Some of the evening gowns will have a fitted bodice and special cut. Last-minute alterations in person can be made, but it's helpful to have a ballpark number to start with."

Resisting the urge to flatten her hands to her breasts required a Herculean effort. "Thirty-four C."

He didn't look away from his iPhone, but a slow sexy smile creased his face. The air between them crackled and her nipples ached inside her strapless pushup. This man was entirely too audacious. And enticing. Finally, he put away his phone and returned his focus to her.

"A new 'princess' wardrobe will be waiting in the morning with enough garments to see you through our first few days of travel. The rest of your clothing for the month will arrive before the end of the week." He thumbed the engagement ring on her finger, nudging the ruby back to the center again.

His simple touch stirred her as much now as his kiss had earlier, and this time they were alone rather than in a ballroom full of onlookers. His gaze fell to her mouth, brown eyes turning lava-dark with desire.

He'd told her the engagement was mutually beneficial for practical reasons, but at the moment she wondered if he had a different agenda. Could he really be so interested in getting her into his bed that he would expose himself to press coverage? That he would want her so much after one meeting was mind-blowing. Who wouldn't be complimented?

Except it also felt so far out of the realm of possibility that she felt conceited for considering it. Revenge seemed a far more logical reason for the seductive gleam he directed at her.

Either way, she needed to keep her guard up at all times. "Thank you. I will be certain the reporter who pens the stories accompanying my photos notes that you have impeccable, princely manners."

"No thanks or credit needed. I won't even notice the expense of a few dresses and 34C bras."

Her fingers curved into a fist under his touch. "I was referring to your consideration in looking after my cat before we leave."

"Again, that has nothing to do with being nice." He enfolded her curled hand in his until it disappeared. "I'm only taking care of loose ends so we can move forward."

This man was such a strong presence he could eclipse a person as fully as his palm covered her hand. "Of course I'll also have to make note in the article that you're bossy."

"I prefer to think I'm a take-charge sort of man."

"You would have made a great general."

He traced from her ring finger around to the vein leading to the pulse in her wrist. "Why do I feel like you're not complimenting me?"

"Don't you worry about how I'll present you in stories once this is over? Photography may be my main focus, but I do write articles on occasion."

The warmth of his clasp seared her skin. They were

just linking fingers, for crying out loud, something as innocent as two teens in a movie theater. But they weren't in some public locale.

They were alone, and she questioned the wisdom of letting him touch her in private. The heated look in his eyes was most definitely anything but innocent.

"You'll be the ex-fiancée. It'll all sound like sour grapes." He released her fist and stood before she could pull away. "Regardless, I don't give a flying f—"

"Right. Got it." She raised both hands. "You don't care what people think of you."

"I only cared about privacy, and now that's a moot point." He walked around the table, stopping beside her and tipping her chin with a knuckle. "So let's get back to talking about how smoking-hot you look regardless of what you wear, and how much better you must look in nothing at all."

She saw this for what it was, a gauntlet moment where she could either back down—or let him know she wasn't a pushover. No dancing around the subject or pretending to ignore his seductive moves to keep some kind of peace. She'd always met life head-on and now wouldn't be any different.

"Stop trying to throw me off balance." She stared at him without flinching or pulling away. "I've kept a steady hand taking pictures through bomb blasts in a war zone and during aftershocks in earthquake rubble. I think I can handle a come-on from you."

A flicker of approval mingled with the desire in his dark eyes at her moxie. And how silly to be excited because she'd impressed him with something other than her cup size. She wasn't interested in the man beyond what he had to offer in a photo op.

Okay, not totally true. Truth be told, just looking at

him turned her on. Hearing his light Spanish accent stoked that a notch. He was a handsome man, and a big-time winner in the genetic gene pool when it came to charisma.

But that didn't mean she intended to act on the attraction.

"I can handle you," she repeated, just as much to reassure herself as to convince him.

"Good, an easy victory isn't nearly as much fun." He reached behind her, his hand coming back with a thick white robe. He passed the folded terry cloth bearing the resort logo to her. "Enjoy your shower."

Kate was naked under the robe.

The terry cloth was thick and long and covered her completely from Duarte's eyes as he lounged in her suite. But deep in his gut, he knew. She wore nothing more.

He went utterly still in his chair by her fireplace. He'd waited for a half hour in her suite, a large room with a sitting area in the bay window, sleigh bed across the room. She stood in the doorway from her bathroom, her fluffy robe accenting the crisp blue-and-white decor. Her wet hair was gathered in a low ponytail draped over one shoulder.

It was longer than he'd expected. He also expected her to demand that he leave. But she simply tucked her feet into the complimentary slippers by the door and padded across the room toward him.

Unflinching, she stared back at him, her eyes sweeping down him as if taking in every detail of his tuxedo shirt open at the neck, dark pants sans cummerbund, feet propped on the ottoman. She stopped alongside him and sank smoothly into the blue checkered chair on the other side of the fireplace. She was fearless.

And magnificent.

She crossed her legs, baring a creamy calf. "What else do we need to cover before facing the world tomorrow?"

The fire crackled and warmed. He'd started the blaze to set a more intimate tone. Except now it tormented him by heating her pale leg to an even more tempting rosy pink. "Let's discuss how we met. You spin mythical stories from a thread of truth. How about take a stab at it by creating our dating history?"

"Hmm..." Her foot swung slowly, slipper dangling from her toes, her yarn jewelry still circling her ankle. "After I broke the story about your family, you confronted me...at my apartment... You didn't want to risk being seen at my office. You know where I live, right? Since you knew to send someone to take care of my cat."

"You're based out of Boston, but travel frequently," he confirmed correctly. "So you just keep a studio apartment."

"Your detectives have done their homework well." Her smile went tight, her plump lips thinning. "Did you already know about Jennifer?"

"No, I only know your address and work history."

Perhaps there he'd dropped the ball. He, above all people, should know how family concerns shaped a person's perspective. Pieces of the Kate puzzle readjusted in his mind, and he resolved to get back to the issue of her sister.

Although Kate's tight mouth let him know he would have to tread warily. "Tell me, Ms. Harper, how does someone who covered the wars in Iraq and Afghanistan end up working for the *Global Intruder?*"

"Downsizing in the newspaper industry." She blinked fast as if working hard not to look away nervously.

"Taking care of your sister had nothing to do with your decisions?" He understood her protectiveness when it came to her sibling. The bond was admirable, but he wouldn't let softer feelings blur his goal.

"Jennifer needs me." Kate picked at the white piping along the club chair.

"There were plenty of people willing to roll out for an assignment at the drop of the hat." Unanswered questions about her career descent now made perfect sense. "By the time you settled your sister, you'd lost out on assignments. Other reporters moved ahead of you. Have I got it right?"

Fire snapped in her eyes as hotly as the flames popping in the fireplace. "How does this pertain to fielding questions about our engagement? If the subject of Jennifer comes up, we'll tell the media it's none of their business."

"Well, damn." He thumped himself on the forehead. "Why didn't my family and I come up with that idea ourselves? To think we hid out and changed our identity for nothing."

"Are you sure we'll be able to convince anyone we even like each other, much less that we're in love?"

He tamped down the anger that would only serve to distract. This woman was too adept at crawling under his skin. "We're only talking about your basic life story. Surely you can trust me with that."

"Give me a good reason why I should trust you with anything. I don't really know you." She toyed with the tip of her damp ponytail, releasing a waft of shower-fresh *woman*. "Perhaps if you would tell me more about your past, I'll feel more comfortable opening up in return."

"Touché," he said softly as a lighthouse horn wailed in the distance. "Instead, we'll move back to creating our dating history."

She dropped her ponytail and stared upward as if plucking the story from the air. "On the day we met, I was wearing khaki pants, a Bob Marley T-shirt, and Teva sandals. You remember it perfectly because you were entranced by my purple toenail polish." Her gaze zipped and locked with his again. "You get bonus points if you remember the polish had glitter. We ended up talking for hours."

"What was *I* wearing?"

"A scowl." She grinned wickedly.

"You sound positively besotted."

She flattened a hand to her chest dramatically, drawing his eyes to the sweet curves of her breasts. "I *swooned*." Kate leaned forward, her robe gaping enough to tease him with a creamy swell but not enough to give him a clear view. "I took your picture because I found you darkly intriguing and the feeling increased when you came to confront me about exposing your identity. The attraction was instantaneous. Undeniable."

"That part will be very easy to remember." His groin tightened the longer he looked at the peekaboo flesh of her generous breasts.

"You wooed me. I resisted, of course." Clasping the neck of her robe closed, she sat back. Had she tormented him on purpose? "But ultimately I fell for you."

"Do tell what I did to convince you." Any edge with Kate would be helpful.

Her grin turned mischievous. "You won me over with your love poem."

He leaned back. "Afraid not."

"I was joking." She toe-tapped his feet, propped and crossed on the ottoman.

"Oh. Okay. I see that now. I'm not artistic." His family also said he lacked a sense of humor, which had never bothered him before, but could prove problematic in dealing with this woman. He needed to turn the tables back in his favor. "I can be romantic without resorting to sappy sonnets."

"Then let's hear how you spin the story of our first date." She waved with a flourish for him to take over. "How did it go?"

"I picked you up in my Jaguar."

Kate crinkled her nose, shaking her head. "Nuh-uh. Too flashy to wow me."

"It's vintage."

"That's better," she conceded.

"And red."

"Even better yet."

He searched his mental catalogue of information about her for the right detail... "I brought you catnip and *cat*viar, instead of flowers and candy."

"You remembered I have a cat?" The delighted surprise in her voice rewarded his effort.

"I remembered everything you told me, although you neglected to mention her name and breed."

"*He* is a gray tabby named Ansel."

"As in Ansel Adams, the photographer. Nice." He filed away another piece of information about the intriguing woman in front of him.

"No flowers and candy at all, though. I'm surprised. I would expect you to be the exotic bouquet and expensive truffle sort."

"Too obvious. I can see you're intrigued by my unusual choice, which makes my point." That little strip of braided yarn she wore told him that Kate had a sentimental side. "Moving on. We ate a catered dinner on my private jet, so as not to attract attention in a restaurant."

"Your airplane? Where were we going?"

"The Museum of Contemporary Photography in Chicago."

"I haven't been there before," she said wistfully.

He vowed then and there to take her before the month was over. "We learned a lot about each other, such as food preferences—" He paused.

"Chili dogs with onions and a thick slice of wedding cake, extra frosting," she answered, toying with the tassel on the tapestry wall hanging behind her. "What about you?"

"Paella for me, a Spanish rice dish." Although he'd never been able to find a chef who could replicate the taste he remembered from San Rinaldo. "And your favorite color?"

"Red. And yours?"

"Don't have one." His world was a clear-cut image of black and white, right and wrong. Colors were irrelevant. "Coffee or tea drinker?"

"Coffee, thick and black served with New Orleans–style beignets."

"We're in agreement on the coffee, churros for me." Now on to the important details. "Favorite place to be kissed?"

She gasped, fidgeting with the tie to her robe. "Not for public knowledge."

"Just want to make sure I get it right when the cameras start. For the record, we kissed on the first date but you wouldn't let me get to second base until—"

"I don't intend for any interview to reach that point and neither will you."

"But we did kiss on our first date." He swung his feet to the floor and leaned forward, elbows on his knees. Closer to her.

"After your display in the ballroom, the whole world knows we've, uh, kissed."

He clamped his fingers around her ankle, over the beaded yarn. "From what I've learned about you tonight, kissing you, touching you, I think you have very sensitive earlobes."

Her pupils widened, her lips parting and for a moment he thought she would sway forward, against him, into him. The memory of her curves pressed to his chest earlier imprinted his memory. How much more mind-blowing the sensation would be bare flesh to flesh.

Kate drew in a shuddering breath. "I think we've learned quite enough about each other for one evening." She crossed her arms just below her breasts. "You should go so I can get some sleep."

The finality in her tone left no room for doubt. He'd pushed her as far as he could for one night. And while he would have preferred to end the evening revealing every inch of her body beneath that robe, he took consolation in knowing he had a month to win her over.

Easing back, he shoved to his feet. Was that regret in her eyes? Good. That would heighten things for them both when he won her over.

Five

The next morning, Kate pulled on her borrowed clothes, made of fabric so fine it felt like she wore nothing at all.

The silk lined linen pants were both warm and whispery. A turtleneck, cool against her skin, still insulated her from the crisp nip in the winter air leaching into her suite. They'd gotten everything right from the size of the clothes to her favored cinnamon-apple fragrance. Had he noticed even that detail about her?

Everything fit perfectly, from the brown leather ankle boots—to her bra. Toying with the clasp between her breasts, she wondered how much he knew about the selections.

All had been brought to her by the resort staff, along with a note, beignets and black coffee. The aftertaste of her breakfast stirred something deeper inside her, a place already jittery at the notion of him envisioning her underwear. He'd listened to her preferences about food choices. He'd remembered.

He'd even come through on his promise to deliver a secured laptop for her to send her photos to Harold Hough, her editor at the *Global Intruder.* Duarte had kept his word on everything he'd promised.

She trailed her fingers over the two packed bags with her other new clothes neatly folded and organized, along with shoes and toiletries. She plucked out a brush and copper hair clamp. What a different world, having anything appear with the snap of his fingers.

Sweeping the brush through her hair, she shook it loose around her shoulders. Excitement twirled in her belly like the snowflakes sifting from the clouds. She scooped up the fur-lined trench and matching suede gloves, wondering where they would go after stopping by her place for her cameras.

How could she want to spend time with a man who, underneath the trappings, was all but blackmailing her? She churned the dichotomy around in her brain until finally resolving to look at this as a business deal. She'd agreed to that deal wholeheartedly out of desperation, and she would make the best of her choice.

Kate stepped into the hall and locked her door behind her. Duarte's note with her breakfast had instructed her to meet him in his office after she ate and dressed.

Pivoting, she nearly slammed into a man who seemed to have materialized out of nowhere.

"Excuse me." She jolted back a step, away from the guy in a dark suit with an even darker glower.

"Javier Cortez—I work for Duarte Medina," he introduced himself, his accent thicker than his boss's. "I am here to escort you to his office." Javier was even more somber than his employer.

Duarte was intense. This guy was downright severe.

Something about his name tugged at her memory—and was that a gun strapped to his belt? "What exactly do you do here for Duarte?"

"I am head of security."

That explained the gun, at least. "Thank you for the help. I don't know my way around the resort yet."

His footsteps thudded menacingly down the Persian runner. "You managed quite well last night."

She winced. He must be the keeper of the video footage from her not-so-successful entrance. Which meant he also likely knew the engagement was a farce. She thumbed the ring and gauged her words.

"Last night was a memorable evening for many reasons, Mr. Cortez."

Pausing outside a paneled wood door, Javier faced her down. Why did he look so familiar? The other two Medina brothers were named Antonio and Carlos, not Javier. Roughly the same age and bearing as Duarte, still Javier didn't look like a relative.

And she couldn't help but notice that while he was undoubtedly handsome, this guy didn't entice her in the least.

"Is this his office?"

"The back entrance. Yes." His arm stretched across it barred her from entering—and parted his jacket enough to put his gun in plain sight. "Betray my friend and you will regret it."

She started to tell him to drop the B-grade-movie melodrama, then realized he was serious. She didn't give ground. Bullies never respected a wimp anyway. "So he tells me."

"This time, *I* am telling you. Know that I will be

watching your every step. Duarte may trust you with your cameras and that secure laptop, but I'm not so easily fooled."

Irritation itched through two dings of the elevator down the hall before she cleared her brain enough to realize what had bothered her about the man's name and why he looked familiar. "You're angry about your cousin getting booted out of royal favor for tipping me off."

His jaw flexed with restraint, his eyes cold. "Alys is an adult. She chose wrong. My cousin was disloyal not only to our family and the Medinas, but she also betrayed our entire country. I'm angry with *her*. Alys must accept responsibility for her actions, and you can feel free to cite me on that in your gossip e-zine."

"Thank you for the quote. I'll be sure they spell your name correctly." She hitched her hands on her hips. "I'm just curious about clarifying one point. If you're only mad at her and realize I was just doing my job, why are you reading me the riot act about not hurting Duarte?"

"Because I do not trust you." Javier stepped closer, his intent obviously to intimidate. "I understand you made your decision for practical reasons. Yes, you were doing your job. Understand, I am doing mine, and I am far more ruthless than you could ever hope to be."

As much as she resented being towered over, she understood and respected the need to protect the people you cared about. Javier might be a bully, but he wasn't just looking out for himself.

"You know what, Javier Cortez? Everybody should have a friend like you."

"Compliments won't work with me." He stared down his sharp nose at her. "Remember, I'll be watching you."

The door swung open abruptly. The security guru jerked upright.

Duarte frowned, looking from one to the other. "Is something wrong here, Javier?"

"Not at all," he answered. "I was only introducing myself to your fiancée."

"Kate?" Duarte asked her, his gaze skeptical.

She stepped in front of Javier and a little too close to Duarte. His hair still damp, she caught a whiff of her faux fiancé's aftershave and a hint of crisp air. Had he already been for a walk outside?

And ouch, how silly to wonder how he'd spent his morning.

A cleared throat behind her reminded Kate of the bodyguard. "Your buddy Javier was just giving me the lowdown on security around here."

As much as she wanted to tell Javier to shove it, the guy had a point. She needed to watch her step.

She couldn't allow herself to be swayed by Duarte's charming images of jet-setting dates and catnip gifts. This was a man who lived with security cameras and ruthless armed guards. He was every bit as driven as she was. She needed to harden her resolve and shore up her defenses if she expected to survive this month unscathed.

Which meant keeping tempting touches to a minimum.

Outside Kate's Boston apartment, Duarte slid inside the limousine, heater gusting full blast. The door closed, locking him in the vehicle with Kate and his frustration over finding her with Javier earlier. Not that he was jealous. He didn't do that emotion. However, seeing them standing close together made him...

Hell, he didn't know what it made him feel, but he didn't like the way his collar suddenly seemed too tight. He swiped the sleet from his coat sleeves.

After they'd taken the ferry from Martha's Vineyard, they'd spent the past couple hours driving through snow turned to sleet on their way to her place. She'd insisted on retrieving her cameras herself, stating she didn't want one of his "people" pawing through her things. He understood the need for privacy and had agreed. He controlled his own travel plans, after all. A few hours' wiggle room didn't pose a problem.

A hand's reach away, Kate sorted through her camera bag she'd retrieved from her tiny efficiency. The bland space where she lived had relayed clearly how little time she spent there.

She looked up from her voluminous black bag as ice and packed snow crunched under the limo's tires. "May I ask what's next on the agenda or are we going to an undisclosed location?"

"I have a private jet fueled and waiting to fly us to D.C. as soon as the weather clears. After we land, we'll stay at one of my hotels." He selected a card from his wallet and passed it to her. "Here's the address, in case you want to let your sister—or the *Intruder*—know."

Not that anyone would get past his security.

He'd bought the nineteenth-century manor home in D.C. ten years ago. With renovations and an addition, he'd turned it into an elite hotel. He catered to the wealthy who spent too much time on the road and appreciated the feeling of an exclusive home away from home while doing business in the nation's capital.

Silently, she pulled out her cell phone from her bag and began texting, her silky hair sliding forward over one shoulder. She was a part of the press. He couldn't forget for a second that he walked a fine line with her.

He needed to be sure she remembered, as well. "Don't make the mistake of thinking Javier is cut from the same cloth as his cousin. You were able to trick Alys, but Javier is another matter."

She kept texting without answering, sleet pinging off the roof. He studied her until she glanced over at him, tight-lipped.

Anger frosted Kate's blue eyes as chilly as the bits of melted sleet still spiking her eyelashes. "For your information, I didn't have to trick your pal Alys. Yes, I approached her about the photo I accidentally snapped of you at Senator Landis's beach house. But *she* came to *me* about your half sister."

Duarte registered her words, but he could only think about her determination, her drive…and her 34C breasts. He wondered what his assistant had chosen for Kate. As much as he wanted to know, checking out the clothes before they were sent to her felt…invasive. Privacy was important.

He understood that firsthand. "You made the contact with Alys when you chased her down about that photo of me with the senator."

"Believe what you want." She changed out the lens on a camera with the twist of her wrist. "I merely traced people in the picture until one of them was willing to give up more information on the mysterious past of a guy who called himself Duarte Moreno."

Hearing how easily someone in his father's inner circle could turn angered him. But it also affirmed what he'd thought during his entire isolated childhood on the island. There was no hiding from the Medina legacy. "You'll be wise to remember how easy it is to misstep. If our secret is out, I'll have no reason to keep you around until the wedding."

A small yellow rag in hand, she cleaned a lens. "One screwup and that's it? No room for mistakes and forgiveness? Everyone deserves an occasional do over."

"Not when the stakes are so high." A single mistake, a break in security, could cost a life. His mother had died and Carlos still carried scars from that day.

"Aren't you curious as to why Alys was willing to sell out your family?"

"The 'why' doesn't matter."

"There, you are wrong." She handled her camera reverently. "The 'why' can matter very much."

"What happened to neutral reporting of the facts?" He hooked a finger along her black camera strap.

"The 'why' can help a good journalist get more information from a source."

"All right, then. Why did Alys turn on us?"

Kate raised the camera to her face, lens pointed in his direction, and when he didn't protest, she clicked.

He forced himself not to flinch, tough to do after so long hiding from having his image captured as if the camera could steal his spirit. "Kate?"

"Alys wanted to be a Medina princess." Kate lowered the camera to her lap. "But how much fun would the tiara be worth if she couldn't show it off to the world? She wanted everyone to know about the Medinas, and my camera made that possible."

"Don't even try to say she had feelings for one of us. She wouldn't have betrayed us if she cared."

"True enough." Her voice drifted off and he could all but see the investigative wheels turning in her mind. "Did *you* love *her?* Is that why you're so edgy today?"

His restlessness had everything to do with Kate and nothing to do with Alys, a woman he considered past history. "What do you think?"

"I believe it must have hurt seeing a trusted friend turn on your family, especially if she meant something more to you."

"I'm not interested in Alys, never was beyond a couple dates. Any princess dreams she may have harbored were of her own making."

In a flash of insight, he realized she was curious about his past relationships, and not as a reporter, but as a woman. Suddenly his frustration over finding her with Javier didn't irritate him nearly as much.

He slid his arm along the back of the leather seat.

"Uh…" Kate jumped nervously. "What do you think you're doing?"

Dipping his face toward her hair, he nuzzled her ear. When she purred softly, he continued, "Kissing my fiancée, or I will be," he said on his way toward her parted lips, "momentarily."

Catching her gasp, his mouth met hers. His hand between her shoulder blades drew her closer. The rigid set of her spine eased and she flowed into him, her lips softening. The tip of her tongue touched his with the first tentative sweep. Then more boldly.

Carefully, he moved her camera from her lap to the seat. He untied her belt and pushed her coat from her shoulders. The turtleneck hugged her body to perfection, the fabric so thin he could almost imagine the feel of her skin under his hands. He cupped her rib cage, just below her breasts. If his thumb just twitched even an inch, he could explore the lush softness pressed against him.

Heat surged through his veins so quickly he could have sworn it would melt the sleet outside. Shivering, she brushed against him, her breasts pebbling against his chest in unmistakable arousal.

Kate's breathy gasp caressed his face and she wriggled closer. "What are we doing?"

"I want to reassure you. You have no worries where Alys is concerned." He swept her hair from her face, silky strands gliding between his fingers, catching on calluses. "You have my complete and undivided attention."

"Whoa, hold on there a minute, Prince Charming." She eased away. "That's quite an ego you're sporting there."

"You wanted to know if I had a relationship with Alys. And you weren't asking for some article. Am I wrong?"

"I'm the one who's wrong. I should have stopped that kiss sooner. I'm not even sure why…" She pulled her coat back over her shoulders. "Last night was a different matter. That display was for the public."

"I had no idea you were into voyeurism."

"Don't be dense."

"I'm complimenting you. I enjoyed that kiss so much I want a repeat."

"To what end?"

He simply smiled.

Her pupils widened in unmistakable arousal even as she scooted away, crossing her arms firmly and defensively across chest. "We made a month-long business deal, and then we walk away. You said sleeping together wasn't a part of the plan unless I asked. And I do not intend to ask. I don't do casual sex."

He eased her tight arms from her chest and looped the trench tie closed again. "Then we'll have to make sure there's nothing casual about it."

Six

Two days later, Kate let the live band's waltz number sweep her away on the dance floor with Duarte in his D.C. hotel. The tuxedoed musicians played a mix of slower show tunes, segueing out of a *Moulin Rouge* hit and into a classic from *Oklahoma*. Duarte's hand linked with hers, his other at her back. Crystal chandeliers dimming, he guided her through the steps with an effortless lead. For the moment, at least, she was content to pass over control and simply enjoy the dazzling evening with her handsome date.

She'd been endlessly impressed by all she'd seen of his restored hotel and this ballroom was no exception. Greco-Roman architectural details mirrored many of the Capital City's earliest buildings. Wide Doric columns soared high to murals painted on the ceilings, depicting characters from classic American literature. Huck Finn stared down at her alongside Rip Van Winkle. Moby Dick rode a wave on another wall.

The black-tie dinner packed with politicians and embassy officials had been a journalistic dream come true. The five-course meal now over, she one-two-threed past a senator partnered with an undersecretary in the State department. Her fingers had been itching all night long to snap pictures, but Duarte had been generous with allowing other photographs while they were in D.C. She had to play by his rules and be patient.

And he'd been open to her sharing tips with her boss at the *Global Intruder*. Duarte had spent the past two days meeting with embassy officials from San Rinaldo and neighboring countries. He'd delivered a press conference on behalf of his family. She'd racked up plenty of tips and images to send on the laptop.

Although, sticky politics had quickly taken a backseat to questions about the fiancée at his side. Kate had to applaud his savvy. He'd been right in deciding an engagement could prove useful as he steered the media dialogue.

The press as a whole was having a field day with the notion of a Medina prince engaged to the woman who'd first broken his cover. Their concocted courtship story packed the blogosphere.

Undoubtedly images of them waltzing together would continue the Cinderella theme in the society pages. Her off-the-shoulder designer dress tonight was a world away from the ill-fitting gown she'd worn when breaking into Duarte's Martha's Vineyard resort. The shimmer of champagne-colored satin slithered over her with each sweeping step, giving her skin a warm glow. Duarte's hand on her back, his even breaths brushing her brow, took that warm glow to a whole new and deeper level.

She glanced up into his dark eyes and saw past the somber air to the thoughtfulness he tried so hard to hide. "Thank you for the clothes and the dinner. You really have come through on what you promised."

"Of course." He swept her toward the outer edges of the dance floor, around a marble pillar, farther from the swell of music. "I gave you my word."

"People lie to the press all the time." People lied period. "I accept it."

"I never expected to meet a woman as jaded as myself." His hand on her back splayed wider, firmer. "Who broke your heart?"

She angled closer, resting her head against his jaw so she wouldn't have to look in his too-perceptive eyes. "Let's not wreck this perfect evening with talk about my past." With talk about her father. "Just because you've got a packed romantic history doesn't mean everyone else does."

Wait! Where had that come from? It seemed they bumped into his old girlfriends around every corner. Not that she cared other than making sure they kept their stories straight about the engagement.

Maybe if she told herself that often enough, she might start believing it. Somewhere over the past few days, she'd started enjoying his presence. She really didn't want him to be a jerk.

"Hmm…" He nuzzled her upswept hair, a loose bundle of fat curls dotted with tiny yellow diamonds, courtesy of a personal stylist brought in for her for the afternoon. "What do you know about my dating history?"

"You're like a royal George Clooney. Except younger." And hotter. And somehow here, with her.

"Did you expect me to be a monk just because I had

to live under the radar?" His hand on her back pressed slightly, urging her closer as the music slowed.

"Best as I can tell from the women I've met during our time in D.C.—" she paused, her brain scrambling with each teasing brush of his body against hers, nothing overt, but just enough to make her ache for a firmer pressure "—you've never had a relationship that lasted more than three months."

His ex-girlfriends had wished her luck, *lots* of luck. Their skepticism was obvious. Women he hadn't dated were equally restrained in their good wishes.

"Would you prefer I led someone on by continuing a relationship beyond the obvious end?"

"Don't you care that you broke hearts?" Money and good looks, too, not fair. And then she realized… "Those women didn't even know you're a prince. You're positively a dangerous weapon now."

Why was she pushing this? Old news wouldn't make for much of a media tip. It shouldn't matter that this man who collected luxury hotels around the country had never committed to a single house, much less a particular woman.

He exhaled dismissively. "Anyone who's interested in me because of my bank balance or defunct title isn't worth your concern. Now can we discuss something else? There's the U.S. ambassador to Spain."

"I've already met him. Thank you." She had nabbed award-winning photos by never backing down. She wouldn't change now. "Didn't it bother you, lying to women about your past?"

"Perhaps that's why I never stayed in a relationship." He tucked their clasped hands closer and flicked her dangling earring. Yellow diamonds in a filigree gold setting tickled her shoulder. "Now there are no more constraints."

Her heart hitched in her chest at his outlandish implication. Even knowing he couldn't possibly be serious, she couldn't resist asking, "Are you trying to seduce me?"

"Absolutely. And I intend to make sure you enjoy every minute of it."

With a quick squeeze of their linked hands, he stepped back. The song faded to an end. He applauded along with the rest of the guests while she stood stunned and tingling.

Only seventy-two hours since she'd climbed onto his balcony and already she was wondering just how much longer she could hold out against Duarte Medina.

Abruptly, Duarte frowned and reached into his tuxedo coat. His hand came back out with his iPhone.

"Excuse me a second." The phone buzzed in his hand again. "Javier? Speak."

As he listened, his frown shifted to an outright scowl. His body tensed and his eyes scanned the room. Kate went on alert. Something was wrong. She looked around, but saw nothing out of the ordinary.

He disconnected with a low curse and slid an arm around her waist. His touch was different this time, not at all seductive, but rather proprietary.

Protective.

"What's wrong?" she asked.

"We need to duck out. Now." He hauled her toward a side exit. "Security alert. We have party crashers."

Duarte hurried Kate the rest of the way down the hall and into the elevator. No one followed, but he wasn't taking any chances or wasting a minute. Even a second's delay could prove catastrophic.

The old-fashioned iron grate rattled shut, then the doors slid closed on the wooden compartment, sealing him inside with Kate and jazz Muzak.

Finally, he had her safely alone, away from cameras, party crashers and the scores of other people wanting a piece of her simply because she wore his ring. Growing up, he'd resented like hell the island isolation his father had imposed on them all. But right now, he wouldn't have minded some of that seclusion.

He stabbed the stop button and reached for his phone to check for text updates from Javier.

"Duarte?" Kate gripped his wrist. "Why aren't we going upstairs?"

"Soon." He needed to ensure her security before he let himself enjoy how easily she touched him now. "We are going to hang out here until Javier gets the lowdown on those party crashers." Duarte scrolled through the incoming texts.

Inching closer, she eyed the corners of the wood elevator suspiciously. The side of her breast brushed his arm. His hand gripped the phone tighter.

Even if they were only in the elevator, he had her all to himself for the first time since he'd seen the shift in her eyes. He'd known she felt the same attraction from the start and seventy-two hours straight spent together had crammed months' worth of dates and familiarity into a short period.

On the dance floor, he'd sensed any residual resistance melting from her spine. However, he couldn't think of that now. He needed to get Kate to a secure location, and then find out how the pair of party crashers had slipped through security.

Picking nervously at the yellow diamond earring, Kate nodded toward his phone. "What's the report? Can we talk in here?"

"Yes." He tucked his phone back into his coat.

"You're sure? No bugs or cameras? Remember, I know how sneaky the press can be."

"This is my hotel, with my security." Although right now his security had suffered a serious breach in the form of two struggling actors seeking to increase their visibility. If the party crashers' confessions were even true. They had every reason to lie. "I stay in my own establishments whenever possible. Javier has two people in custody. He's checking their story and also making sure there aren't more people involved. Luckily, the initial pair never made it past the coat check."

"Sounds like Javier earned his Christmas bonus tonight."

"He's a valuable member of my staff."

Sighing, she sagged onto the small bench lining the back of the elevator, red velvet cushion giving slightly beneath her. "So the crisis is over?"

"We should know soon. Javier is questioning them directly." As security concerns eased, his other senses ramped into overdrive, taking in the scent of Kate's hair, the gentle rise and fall of her chest in her off-the-shoulder gown. "Anything more?"

Possibilities for that bench marched through his mind with unrelenting temptation.

"No, nothing, well, except you confuse me. You've been such a prince—in a good way—for the past three days. Then you go all autocratic on me." Her head fell back against the mirror behind her. "Never mind. It doesn't matter. A grumpy prince is easier to resist than a charming prince."

He stepped closer. "You're having trouble resisting me?"

Her fingers dug into the crushed velvet. "You have a certain appeal."

"Glad to hear it." He liked the way she didn't gush with overblown praise. Duarte sat beside her.

"What are you doing?"

"Waiting for the okay from Javier." He slid his arm around her shoulders and nuzzled her neck.

"What about the mirror? Are you sure it's not a two-way?" she asked but didn't pull back.

"Thinking like a journalist, I see. Smart." He grazed his knuckles along her bared collarbone, eliciting a sexy moan from her.

Flattening her hands against his chest, she dug her fingers in lightly. Possessively? "I'm thinking like the paranoid fiancée of a prince. Unless your whole intent is for someone to snap pictures of us making out in an elevator. I guess that would go a long way toward persuading the public we're a happily engaged couple."

"What I want to do with you right now goes beyond simple making out, and you can be sure, I don't want anyone seeing you like that except me. I pay top dollar to my security people. Everything from my phones, to my computers, to my hotels—this is *my* domain," he declared, his mouth just over hers. "Although you're right in that it's always wise to double-check the mirrors."

He reached behind her and ran his fingers along the frame. "This one is hung on the elevator wall rather than mounted in it. And when you press against the pane..." He angled toward her until their bodies met, her back to the glass. "Hear that? Not a hollow thump. A regular mirror for me to see the beautiful curve of your back."

"Duarte…" She nipped his lower lip.

"Not that I need to see your reflection when the real deal right in front of me is so damn mesmerizing," he growled.

Sliding his hands down, he cupped her waist and shifted her around until she straddled his lap. Champagne-colored satin pooled around them, her knees on either side of him. His groin tightened. The need to have her burned through him.

And then she smiled.

Her soft cool hands cupped either side of his face and she slanted her lips more firmly across his. Just as she gave no quarter in every word and moment of her day, she demanded equal time here and now. He was more than happy to accommodate.

Liquid heat pumped through him as finally he had unfettered access to her mouth. Champagne and strawberries from their dinner lingered. He was fast becoming drunk on the taste of Kate alone. Her fingers crawled under his coat, digging into his back, urgent, insistent.

Demanding.

He thrust his hand in her hair. Tiny diamonds *tink, tink, tinked* from her updo onto the floor.

"Duarte," she mumbled against his mouth.

"We'll find them later." To hell with anything but being with her. He couldn't remember when he'd ached so much to be inside a woman. This woman. He'd known her for three intense days that felt a lot longer than his three-month relationships of the past.

Of course he'd never met anyone like Kate.

His phone buzzed in his coat pocket. She stiffened against him. His phone vibrated again, her fingers between the cell and his chest, so the sensation buzzed through her and into him. She wriggled in his lap. He throbbed in response, so hard for her that he couldn't think of anything else.

"Ignore the phone." He gathered her closer, not near enough with the bunching satin of her evening gown between them.

"The call could be important," she said, regret tingeing her voice as she cupped his face and kissed him quickly again. "It could be Javier with an update. Or something even more important," she insisted between quick nibbles. "You said your father is sick. You don't want to be sorry you ignored a message."

Her words slowly penetrated his passion-fogged brain. What had he been thinking? Of course that was the whole point. Kate had a way of scrambling rational thought.

He pulled out his phone and checked the screen. His gut clenched with dread.

"Duarte?" Kate asked, sliding to sit beside him. "Is everything okay?"

"It's my brother Antonio." He reached for the elevator button, already preparing himself for the worst—that their father had died. "Let's go to our suite. I need to call him back."

Standing in her walk-in closet that rivaled the size of her studio apartment, Kate stepped out of her princess gown and hung it up carefully among the rest of her extravagant wardrobe. Another elaborate fiction, covering up the sham of her engagement with layers of beaded and embroidered fabrics. She smoothed the front of tonight's dress, releasing a whiff of Duarte's cedar scent and memories of the elevator.

As they'd returned to the suite, Duarte had asked

for privacy for his conversation with his brother and suggested she change clothes. Her heart ached to think what he might be hearing now. She wanted to stand beside him and offer silent comfort. Without question, the proud prince wouldn't stand for any overt signs of sympathy. Apparently he saved unrestrained emotions for elevator encounters.

Her body hummed with the memory of embracing him, straddling his lap with the hard press of his arousal evident even through the folds of her dress. Warm air from the vent whispered over her skin as she stood in her matching champagne-colored underwear with nothing more than diamond earrings and a lopsided updo.

How different the evening might have been if the call hadn't come through. She wouldn't have stopped at just a kiss. Right now they could have been living out her fantasy of making love in an elevator.

Or here, in her room, with him peeling off her thigh-high silk stockings. What came next for them now? Would they be leaving right away? Or staying overnight?

She was used to pulling up stakes in a heartbeat for a story. In fact, she kept a change of clothes in her camera case for just such occasions. A camera case that wasn't monogrammed or even made of real leather, for that matter. She was in over her head playing make-believe with a real live prince.

Her cell phone rang from across the room, and she almost jumped out of her skin. Oh, God. Her sister. They hadn't spoken today and Kate had promised. She snatched up an oversized T-shirt from the top of her camera case and yanked it over her head as she sprinted across the room.

She scooped her ringing phone from the antique dresser without looking at the screen. "Hello? Jennifer?"

"'Fraid not," answered her editor from the *Global Intruder*.

Harold Hough kept the e-zine afloat through his dogged determination. She should have known she couldn't avoid him for long.

"Is there some emergency, boss? It's a little late to be calling, don't you think?"

"You're a tough lady to reach now that you're famous. Hope you haven't forgotten us little people."

Sagging on the end of the bed, she puffed out her cheeks with a hefty sigh while she weighed her words. "I explained that my fiancé is fine with me talking to you. I will relay more snippets when Duarte and I have discussed what we're comfortable with the world knowing."

Resentment scratched inside her. Thank God she hadn't told him about her plans to sneak into Duarte's Martha's Vineyard resort. As far as Harold knew, she'd been hiding a relationship with Duarte these past few months and now was attempting to control the fallout with her leaks to him. And she sure wasn't going to tell him about a surprise call from Duarte's brother.

She stared at her closed door, her heart heavy for Duarte and what he might be facing in that conversation.

Harold's voice crackled over the line. "But you were at that exclusive embassy dinner tonight. I've already heard rumblings about some party crashers. I'd hoped to get more pictures from you. Did you receive my latest email tonight? Is there something you're not telling me?" he ended suspiciously.

"Have I ever been anything but honest? I've worked my tail off for the *Intruder*." She paused to apply a little pressure in hopes Harold would back off. "So hard, in fact, maybe I need a vacation."

Tucking the phone against her shoulder, she rolled down a thigh-high stocking while waiting for Harold's response.

"Right, you're distancing yourself from the *Intruder*." His chair squeaked in the background and she could picture him leaning back to grab a pack of gum, his crutch to help him through giving up cigarettes. "You've forgotten I'm the one who made it possible for you to pay your bills."

She rolled off the other stocking, back to her pre-Cinderella self in a familiar baggy T-shirt. "You know I'm grateful for the chance you gave me at the *Intruder*. I appreciate how flexible you've been with my work schedule." No question, she would have been screwed without this job. And she would still need it if things fell apart with Duarte. "I hope you'll remember the information I've shared exclusively with you."

"And I trust you'll remember that I know plenty about you, Ms. Harper." His voice went from lighthearted slimy to laser sharp. "If I don't get the headlines I need, I can send one of my other top-notch reporters to interview your sister. After all, you of all people should know that even royalty can't keep out an *Intruder* reporter."

Seven

Phone in hand, Duarte paced across the sitting area between the two bedrooms. While not as large as his Martha's Vineyard quarters, this suite would still accommodate him and Kate well enough for a few days.

If they even stayed in Washington, D.C., after this conversation with his youngest brother.

Duarte's restless feet took him to the blazing hearth. "How high is his fever?" he asked Antonio—Tony. "Do they know the source of the infection?"

They'd only recently learned that their father had suffered damage to his liver during his escape from San Rinaldo. Enrique had caught hepatitis during his weeks on the run in poor living conditions. His health had deteriorated over the years until their perpetually private father couldn't hide the problem from his children any longer.

"His fever's stabilized at 102, but he's developed pneumonia," Tony answered. "In his weakened condition, they fear he might not be able to fight it off."

"What hospital is he in?" He knelt to stoke the fire in the hearth. Windows on either side of the mantle revealed the night skyline, the nation's capital getting hammered by a blizzard. "Where are you?"

"We're all still at the island, not sure yet when we'll go back to Galveston." His brother's fiancée had a young son from her first marriage. "He's insisting on staying at his clinic, with his own doctors. The old man says they've kept him alive this long, so he trusts them."

Frustrated, Duarte jabbed the poker deeper into the logs, sparks showering. The other suites had gas fireplaces, but he preferred the smell of real wood burning. It reminded him of home—San Rinaldo, not his father's Florida island fortress. "Damn foolhardy, if you ask me. Our father's an agoraphobic, except his 'house' is that godforsaken island."

Tony sighed hard on the other end of the phone. "You may not be far off in your estimation, my brother."

"Okay, then. I'll scrap our next stop, and we'll head straight to the island instead once the snowstorm here clears." He hadn't planned to take Kate there for a few more weeks, but he wasn't ready to leave her behind. "Maybe meeting my charming new fiancé will give him a boost."

"He seemed to take heart from the wedding plans Shannon and I have been making." Tony had proposed only a couple weeks ago, but the pair didn't want to wait to tie the knot.

Duarte had been surprised they chose the island chapel for the ceremony, but Tony had pointed out that place offered the best security from the prying paparazzi. Good thing they'd been amenable to Duarte's suggestion of one reporter for a controlled press release. The *Intruder* wouldn't have been his first choice—or even a fiftieth choice—of outlets for such an important family event, but he'd resigned himself on that point since Kate would serve as the press envoy.

And if he could make a better job open up for her? He cut that thought short.

When Antonio got married at the end of the month, Kate would walk away with her pictures and her guaranteed top-dollar feature. Why should her leaving grate this much? He'd only known her a few days. Tony had dated his fiancée for months and everyone considered their engagement abrupt.

Duarte replaced the iron poker in the holder carefully rather than risk ramming the thing through the fireplace. "Congratulations, my brother," he said, standing, his eyes trained on his fiancée's door, "and I look forward to telling you in person as soon as Kate and I arrive."

"Be happy for yourself, too. Maybe this will help the old man get back on his feet again, then you can ditch the fake engagement."

"What makes you think it's fake?" Now why the hell had he said that?

"Hey now, I know we don't hang out every Friday, but we do communicate and I'm fairly sure you would have told me if you were seriously seeing someone, especially the individual who exposed our cover to the whole world."

"Maybe that's why I didn't tell you. Hooking up with Kate isn't the most logical move I've ever made." That was an understatement, to say the least. But he'd committed to this path, and he didn't intend to back away. "If I'd asked for your opinion you might not have given the answer I wanted to hear."

"Perhaps you have a point there." Tony's laughter faded. "So you really kept this relationship a secret for months? You've actually fallen for someone?"

Bottom line, he should tell Antonio about the setup. He and his brothers didn't live close by. They'd only had each other growing up, which led them to share a lot, trust only each other.

Yet, for some reason he couldn't bring himself to spill his guts about this. "As I said, we're engaged. Wait until you meet her."

"Hanging out with reporters has never been high on my list of fun ways to spend an evening. You sure you're not just looking to poke the old man in the eye?"

Dropping into an armchair and propping a foot on the brocade sofa, he considered Tony's question to see if deep down there was some validity, then quickly dismissed the possibility. It gave his father too much control over his life.

Being with Kate appeared to be more complex than some belated rebellion against his dad. "He will be charmed by her no-B.S. attitude. What's the word from Carlos?"

Their oldest brother kept to himself even more than their father did, immersed in his medical practice rather than on some island. It could well be hours before they heard from Carlos, given the sorts of painstaking reconstructive surgeries he performed on children.

"He's his regular workaholic self. Says he'll get to the island for the wedding, and that he will call Dad at the island clinic. God, I hope the old man can hold on long enough for Carlos to decide he can leave his patients. I'd considered moving up the wedding, but..."

"Enrique insists plans stay in place." His father was stubborn, and he didn't like surprises. For security purposes he preferred life remain as scheduled as possible. Life threw enough curveballs of its own.

Tony rambled on with updates about travel and wedding details. Duarte started to rib his brother over mentioning flower choices for the bride's bouquet—

Across the suite, Kate walked through the door in a knee-length nightshirt. His brain shut down all other thoughts and blood surged south.

"My brother," Duarte interrupted. "I'll get back to you later about my travel plans. I need to hang up."

Kate twisted her hair into a wet rope and hurried barefoot into the sitting area connecting her bedroom to Duarte's.

Almost certainly she should have gone straight to sleep after her conversation with Harold. Except her editor's threat of plastering Jennifer's picture all over a tabloid story sent bile frothing up Kate's throat. She'd played it cool on the phone while reminding Harold of how much she could deliver. Then she'd cut the conversation short rather than risk losing her temper.

Before she could think, she'd rushed to the door, knowing only that she needed the reassurance of Duarte's unflappable calm.

Setting aside his iPhone, he kept his eyes firmly planted on her. "I'm sorry my assistant forgot to order nightwear. The hotel does supply complimentary robes."

"Your assistant didn't forget. This belongs to me. I had it tucked away in my camera case." Kate tugged the hem of her well-worn sleep shirt down to her knees. A picture of a camera marked the middle, words below stating *Don't Be Negative*. "Did everything go all right with your phone call?"

Hopefully his was less upsetting than hers.

"My father has taken a turn for the worse." His body rippled with tension, his hands gripping the carved wood arms of his manor chair. "He has developed pneumonia. And yes, you can leak that to the press if you wish."

Her heart ached that he had to suspect her motives when she only wanted to comfort him. He seemed so distant in his tux against the backdrop of formal damask wallpaper. She searched for the right words to reach him.

"I wasn't thinking about my job. I was asking because you look worried." Seeing the shutters fall, Kate padded past the brocade sofa to the fireplace. She held her chilly hands in front of the blaze. "What do you plan to do?"

"Let's talk about something else."

Like what? She wasn't in the mood for superficial discussions about art. How long could they shoot the breeze about the oil paintings in her room, or the lithographs in his? She'd noticed sailing art in his Martha's Vineyard quarters. Maybe there could be something to those lighter conversations, and certainly she could use the distraction from worries about Jennifer.

"Hey," Duarte said softly from behind her.

She hadn't even heard him move.

The cedar scent of his aftershave sent her mind swirling with memories of how close they'd come to having sex in the elevator. She'd wanted him so much. The fire he'd stirred simmered still, just waiting to be rekindled. She was surprised to find herself with him so soon after. Had she come back in here purposely?

Had she used her frustration over the call from Harold as an excuse to indulge what she wanted?

She looked over her shoulder at him. "Yes?"

Or perhaps she meant *Yes!*

"Is something wrong? You seem upset."

How had this gone from his concerns to hers? Was he avoiding the subject because he didn't trust her? She decided to follow his lead for now and circle back around to discussing Enrique later.

"I'm just worried about Jennifer." She stared back at the fire. "And what will happen if the press decides to write something about her. I have to admit, it's more complicated than I expected, being on the other side of the camera lens."

His angular face hardened with determination. "No one will get past my security people to your sister. I promise."

If only it could be that simple. Nothing was simple about the achy longing inside her. "You and I both know I can't count on your protection long-term."

"After you publish those wedding photos, you'll be able to afford to hire your own security team."

No wonder he didn't trust her. She'd been chasing him down for photos from the start with no thought to the implications for his family. And now her family, as well. She was responsible for putting Jennifer in the crosshairs. Her emotions raw, Kate shivered.

His arms slid around her. "Do you need a robe?"

The cedar scent of his aftershave wrapped around her as temptingly as his hold.

"Is the shirt that ugly?" She looked back at him, attempting to make light, tough to do when she wanted to bury her face in his neck and inhale, taste, *take*.

"You look beautiful in whatever you wear." He eyed

her with the same onyx heat she'd seen during their elevator make-out moment. "I was only worried you might be cold."

"I'm, uh, plenty warm, right now, thank you."

His eyes flamed hotter. The barely banked craving spread throughout her. She couldn't hold back the flood of desire and she swayed toward him. Duarte's arms banded around her in a flash, hauling her toward him.

She met him halfway. Her arms looped around his neck, she opened her mouth and herself to him, to this moment. She couldn't remember when she'd been so attracted to someone so fast, but then nothing about this situation with Duarte qualified as normal.

The warm sweep of his tongue searched her mouth as he engaged her senses. He gathered up her hair in his hands, his fingers combing, massaging, seducing. She pressed closer, his pants against her bare legs a tempting abrasion that left her aching for closer contact. She stroked her bare foot upward, just under the pants hem along his ankle. Hunger gnawed at her insides.

Without breaking contact, he yanked at his loose tux tie and tossed it aside, leaving no doubts where they were headed. Her life was such a mess on so many levels, she couldn't bring herself to say no to this, to taking a few hours of stolen pleasure.

Her fingers crawled down the fastenings, sending studs and cuff links showering onto the floor like her hairpins in the elevator. She tore at his shirt. Finesse gave way to frenzy in her need to verify her memories of him undressing that first night. He took his hands from her long enough to flick aside the starched white cotton in a white flag of mutual surrender.

She peeled off his undershirt, bunching warm cotton in her hands and revealing his hard muscled chest.

The chandelier hanging from a ceiling medallion cast a mellow glow over his chest. He didn't need special photographer's lighting to make his bronzed body look good.

Duarte was a honed, toned *man*.

Kate swayed into him. Her stolen glance when he'd undressed had let loose butterflies in her stomach. Being able to look her fill fast-tracked those butterflies through her veins.

And his body called to her touch as much as it lured her eyes.

Entranced, she tapped down his chest in a rainfall path. Every light contact with the swirls of dark hair electrified the pads of her fingers. Pausing, she traced the small oval birthmark above his navel, an almost imperceptible darkening. Seeing it, learning the nuances of him, deepened the intimacy.

Her fingers fell to his pants.

Duarte covered her hands with his, stopping her for the moment. "We can stop this, if you wish. I don't want any question about why we're together if we take this the rest of the way. This has nothing to do with your job or my family."

Pulling her face back, she stared into his eyes. "No threat of charging me with breaking and entering?"

Even as she jokingly asked him, she knew in her heart he never would have pursued that angle. If he'd wanted to go that route, he would have done so at the start. Somehow, this attraction between them had caught him unaware, too.

He winced. "I want to sleep with you, no mistake about it." The hard length of him pressing against her stomach proved that quite well. "Now that it appears you're in agreement, I need to be sure you're here of your own free will. You have enough information and pictures to set yourself up for life. There's the door."

She could walk now. He was right. Except her life would never return to normal, not after the past few days. Leaving now versus in the morning or three weeks from now wouldn't make any difference for Jennifer.

But having tonight with Duarte felt like everything to Kate. "I'm a little underdressed to leave, don't you think?"

His hot gaze tracked over her, cataloguing every exposed inch and rousing a fiery response in its wake.

Bringing their clasped hands up between them, he kissed her wrists. "I'm serious, in case you hadn't noticed."

"It's tough to miss." She met and held his intense eyes. "Although in case you didn't know it, I'm serious, too."

"When did you figure out I was never going to turn over that tape to anyone?"

"A few minutes ago." Hearing Harold's threat against Jennifer, Kate realized what real evil sounded like. Duarte was tough, but he wasn't malicious. If he'd wanted to prosecute her, he would have done so up-front from the start.

She kissed him once, hard, before pulling back. "No more talking about anything outside the two of us in this suite. I need to be with you tonight, just you and me together in a way that has nothing to do with your last name or any contacts I may have. This is completely private."

"Then there's only one last thing to settle." His hands stroked down her sides until he cupped her hips. "Your bed or mine?"

She considered the question for a second before deciding. "I don't want to engage some power play. Let's meet here, on somewhat neutral ground."

Aside from the fact that they were in his hotel, the symbolism of not choosing one bed over the other still worked for her. She waited for his verdict.

"I'm good with that." He burrowed his hands under her T-shirt, whipping it up and off until she wore nothing but the champagne-colored satin strapless bra and matching panties.

The yellow diamond and filigree gold earrings teased her shoulders.

Like the sweep of Duarte's appreciative gaze. And for some wonderful reason, this hot-as-hell prince was every bit as turned on looking at her as she was looking at him.

She reached, half believing she'd fallen asleep back in her room and was dreaming. Beyond that, what if she'd somehow imagined the magnetic shimmer while kissing him in the elevator?

Her fingers connected with his chest and—*crackle*. A tingle radiated up her arm. This was real. He was real. And tonight was theirs.

This time when she reached for the fastening on his pants, he didn't stop her. His opening zipper echoed in the room along with the *pop, pop* of sparks in the fireplace. He toed off his shoes and socks as she caressed his pants down.

His hands made fast work of her bra and panties. "And now we're both wearing nothing."

He guided her toward him and pressed bare flesh to flesh. They tumbled back onto the sofa in a tangle of arms and legs. She nipped along his strong jaw, the brocade rough against her back, his touch gentle along her sides then away.

Following his hand, she saw him reach into the end table and come back with a condom. Thank goodness at least one of them was thinking clearly enough to take care of birth control. A momentary flash of fear swept through her at how much he affected her.

Then all thoughts scattered.

The thick pressure of him between her legs, poised and ready, almost sent her over the edge then and there. Her breath hitched as she worked to regain control. He thrust deep and full, holding while she adjusted to the newness of him, of them linked. She arched into the sensation, taking him farther inside her. Fingernails sinking deep half moons into his shoulders, she held on to the moment, held back release.

He kept his weight off her with one hand on the back of the couch, the other tucked under her. She rolled her hips under his and he took the cue, resuming the dance they'd started earlier, first in the ballroom, then in the elevator and now taking it to the ultimate level they'd both been craving.

Cedar and musk scented the air, and she buried her face deeper into his shoulder to breathe in the erotic blend. He kissed, nipped and laved his way up to her earlobe, his late-day beard rasping against her jaw. Her every nerve tingled with the memory of that first night in Martha's Vineyard when he'd stroked up her neck. She should have known then she wouldn't hold out long against the temptation to experience all of him.

Control shaky, she wrapped her legs around his waist and writhed harder, faster. Her knee bumped against the back of the sofa, unsettling their balance. She flung out her arms, desperate to hold on to to him, hold on to the moment.

"I've got you," he growled in her ear as they rolled from the brocade couch.

He twisted so his back hit the floor, cushioning her fall. He caught her gasp of surprise and thrust inside her. Her hair streamed over him as she straddled his hips, rug bristly under her knees. He cupped her bottom, guiding her until she recaptured their rhythm.

Were his hands shaking ever so slightly? She looked closer and saw tendons straining in his neck with restraint.

She braced herself, palms against his chest. Delicious tremors rippled up her arms as his muscles twitched and flexed with her caresses. His hands slid around and over her again. He cradled her breasts, teasing and plucking her to tightened peaks that pulled the tension tighter throughout.

Her head lolled and her spine bowed forward. Each thrust of his hips sent her hair teasing along her back. In a distant part of her mind, she heard his husky words detailing all the times he'd watched and wanted her. She tried to answer, truly did, but her answer came out in half-formed phrases until she gave up talking and just moved.

He traced her ribs, working his way down to her waist, over her stomach. Lower. He slid two fingers between them, slickening her taut bundle of aching nerves. She doubted she needed the help to finish, but enjoyed his talented touch all the same.

Carefully, precisely, he circled his thumb with the perfect pressure, taking her so close then easing back, only to nudge her closer.

She gasped out and didn't care how loud. She simply rode the pulsations rocking through her. He gripped her hips again, his hold firmer as he thrust a final time. His completion echoed with hers, sending a second round of lights sparking behind her eyelids and cascading around her until she went limp in the aftermath.

Sagging on top of him, she sealed their sweat-slicked bodies skin to skin. His hands stroked over her hair, his chest pumping beneath hers. She should move and she would, as soon as her arms and legs worked again.

She gazed at him in the half light, her eyes taking in the strong features of his noble lineage. God, even here in his arms she couldn't escape reminders of his heritage, his wealth. She was in so far over her head.

Being with him was different in a way she feared she could never recapture again. Would the rest of her life be spent as a second-best shadow?

And if he made this much of an impact in less than a week, how much more would he change her life if she dared spend the rest of the month with him?

Eight

Yellow moon sinking out of sight, Duarte cradled a sleeping Kate to his chest and carried her to his room. They hadn't spoken after their impulsive tangle. Instead, they'd simply moved closer to the fire for a slower, more thorough exploration. Afterward, she had dozed off in his arms.

Her legs dangled as he carried her. The simple yarn-and-bead-braided string stayed around her ankle. He'd asked her once why she never took it off. She'd told him Jennifer made it as a good luck charm. He didn't consider himself the sentimental type, but he couldn't help but be moved. That she wore the gift even when her sister wouldn't have known otherwise revealed more about her than anything she'd said or done since they'd been together.

Elbowing back the covers, he settled her on the carved four-poster bed and pulled the thick comforter over her.

He eyed the door. He should check his messages and make plans for a morning flight out to see his father, but his feet stayed put.

The allure of watching Kate sleep was too strong. He sat on the edge of the bed, *his* bed. Her hair splayed over the plump pillow, and his hands curved at the memory of silky strands sliding between his fingers.

He'd gotten what he wanted. They'd slept together. He should be celebrating and moving on. Except from the moment he'd been buried inside her, he'd known. Just once with Kate wouldn't be enough.

Already, he throbbed to have her again. The image of her bold and uninhibited over him replayed in his brain. He could watch her all night long.

Why hadn't he told her about going to the island when she'd walked in the room? The truth itched up his spine. After their impulsive kiss in the elevator, he'd sensed they were close to acting on the attraction. But he'd needed her to want him as much as he wanted her. He'd offered her a free pass to walk with all her photos and held back telling her about his imminent trip to see his father.

Now he knew. There was no mistaking her response. And instead of making things easier, his thoughts became more convoluted.

Kate rolled to her back, arm flung out in groggy abandon. Her lashes fluttered and she stared up at him, her eyes still purple-blue with foggy passion. "What time is it?"

"Just after four in the morning."

"Any further word about your father?" She sat up, sheet clutched to her chest her hair tumbling down her shoulders.

"Nothing new." He swallowed hard at the thought of

a world without his father's imposing presence. Time
to invite her into a private corner of his life ahead of
schedule. "But I'm putting the rest of the trip around
the U.S. on hold to see my father first…just in case."

"That's a good idea." She squeezed his knee lightly.
"You don't want to have regrets from waiting."

Resisting the urge to touch her proved impossible. He
stroked a silken lock from her shoulder and lingered.
As much as he wanted her here, he had to know. "My
offer for you to take your pictures and walk away free
and clear still stands."

Her hand slid from his knee, her eyes wary. "Are you
telling me to go?"

Exhaling hard, he gripped her shoulders. "Hell, no. I
want you right where you are. But you need to know that
when we leave for the island, your life will be changed
forever. Becoming a part of the Medina circle alters the
way people treat you, even after you walk away, and not
always in a good way."

Sheet still clutched to her chest, she studied him before answering. "I have one question."

His gut clenched. Could he really follow through on
letting her go while the scent of her still clung to his
skin? "Okay, then. That would be?"

"What time do we leave?"

Relief slammed through him so hard he wondered
again how this woman could have crawled under his
skin so deeply in such a short time. Not that he intended
to turn her away. In fact, he even had an idea of how
to make her life at the island easier. "We'll go in the
morning, once the ice storm has cleared."

Jet engines whispering softly through the sky, Kate
snuggled closer to Duarte's chest. Their clothes were

scattered about the sleeping cabin in the back of the airplane.

Ten minutes after takeoff, she'd snapped photos of him, thinking the well-equipped aircraft with both a bedroom and an office would provide an interesting window into the Medina world. But she'd found her photographer's eye less engaged with his surroundings. Instead she'd increasingly closed in on his face as if she could capture the essence of him just by looking. Too soon, seeing him through the lens hadn't been enough and they'd reached for each other simultaneously, leaving their seats for the private bedroom. Yes, she was using sex to avoid thinking, and she suspected Duarte was, as well.

Tension rippled through his lean muscled body, and she could certainly empathize. Life had been spiraling out of control for her since they'd met.

And now they were winging to some unknown island. Shades covered all the windows so she didn't know if they were traveling over land or water. Duarte had told her the clothes appropriate for the "warmer climate" would be waiting.

What a mess she'd made of things. How was she supposed to report on a man she'd slept with? Should she have taken his offer to walk away?

Her fingers curled around his bare hip, his body now so intimately familiar to her. How much longer could she avoid weightier issues?

Duarte sketched the furrows in her brow. "What's bothering you?"

"Nothing," she said. She wasn't ready to let him know how being with him rocked her focus. Better to distract him. "I've never made love in a plane before."

"Neither have I." His fingers trailed from her brow to tap her nose. "You look surprised."

"Because I am." She expected this man had done all sorts of things she couldn't imagine. "I would have thought during all those three-month relationships, you would have joined the mile-high club at some point."

"You seem to have quite a few preconceived notions about me. I thought journalists were supposed to be objective."

"I am. Most of the time. You're just... Hell, I don't know."

He was different, but telling him that would give him too much power over her. Was she being unfair to Duarte out of her own fear? Was she making assumptions based on an image of a privileged playboy prince?

Swinging her feet off the bed, she plucked her underwear from floor.

Duarte stroked her spine. "Tell me about the man who broke your trust."

"It's not what you think." She pulled on her panties and bra. Where was her dress? And why was she letting his question rattle her? "I haven't had some wretched breakup or bad boyfriend."

"Your father?" Duarte said perceptively as he pulled on his boxers.

Kate slipped her kimono-sleeve dress over her head and swept it smooth before facing Duarte again. "He isn't an evil man or an abuser. He just...doesn't care." Parental indifference made for a deep kind of loneliness she couldn't put to words. Only through her camera had she been able to capture the hollow echo. "It doesn't matter so much for me, but Jennifer doesn't understand. How could she? He cropped himself right out of the family picture."

"Where is he now?" He stepped into his slacks and reached for his chambray shirt.

"He and his new wife have moved to Hawaii, where he can be sure not to bump into us."

"The kind to send his checks as long as he doesn't have to invest anything of himself?"

She stayed quiet, tugging on her leather knee boots.

His hand fell on her shoulder. "Your father does send help, right?"

Bitter words bubbled up her throat. "When Jennifer turned eighteen, he signed over his rights and all responsibility. They were going to put her in the state hospital since she can't live on her own. I couldn't let that happen, so I stepped in."

Duarte sat beside her, taking her hand lightly, carefully. "Have you considered taking him to court?"

"Leave it alone." She flinched away from him and the memories. "Bringing him back into her life only gives him the option to hurt her more than he already has. Jennifer and I will be fine. We'll manage. We always do."

Duarte cursed low. "Still, he should be helping with her care so you don't have to climb around on ledges snapping photos to pay the bills."

"I would do anything for her."

"Even sleep with me."

His emotionless voice snapped her attention back to his face. The coldness there chilled her skin. Confusion followed by shock rippled through her. Did he really believe she could be that calculating? Apparently what they'd shared wasn't as special to him if he thought so poorly of her.

Hurt to the core, she still met his gaze dead-on. "I'm here now because I want to be."

He didn't back down, his face cool and enigmatic. "But would you have slept with me to take care of her?"

And she'd thought she couldn't ache more. "Turn the plane around. I want to go back."

"Hey, now—" he held up his hands "—I'm not judging you. I don't know you well enough to make that call, which is why I'm asking questions in the first place."

Some of the starch flaked from her spine. Hadn't she thought the same thing herself, wondering about ways she may have misjudged him? "Fair enough."

"Has your father called you because of the publicity surrounding your engagement?" he asked, his eyes dark and protective. "People develop all sorts of, uh, creative crises when they think they can gain access to a royal treasure trove."

"I haven't heard a word from him." Although now that Duarte had given her the heads-up, she would be sure to let voice mail pick up if her father did phone. "Other than the obligatory holiday greeting, we haven't heard so much as a 'boo' from him. I guess that's better than having to explain his dropping in and out of our lives."

His hand slid up into her hair, cradling her head. "Your sister is lucky to have you."

"Jennifer and I are lucky to have each other." Kate stood abruptly, refusing to be distracted by his seductive touch.

This conversation reminded her too well that they knew precious little about each other. She'd known her jerk of a father all her life and still she'd been stunned when he dumped his special-needs daughter without a backward glance. What hurtful surprises might lurk under Duarte's handsome surface?

Watching her through narrowed eyes, Duarte pulled on his shoes and gestured her back toward the main cabin. "We'll have to put this conversation on hold. We should be landing soon. Would you like your first glance of the island?"

"The secrecy ends?"

"Revealing the specific location isn't my decision to make." He opened the window shade.

Hungry for a peek at where Duarte had grown up, she buckled into one of the large leather chairs and stared outside. An island stretched in the distance, nestled in miles and miles of sparkling ocean. Palm trees spiked from the landscape, lushly green and so very different from the leafless snowy winter they'd left behind. A dozen or so small outbuildings dotted a semicircle around a larger structure, what appeared to be the main house.

A white mansion faced the ocean in a U shape, constructed around a large courtyard with a pool. Details were spotty but she would get an up-close view soon enough of the place where Enrique Medina had lived in seclusion for over twenty-five years, a gilded cage to say the least. Even from a distance, she couldn't miss the grand scale of the sprawling estate, the unmistakable sort that housed royalty.

Engines whining louder, the plane banked, lining up with a thin islet alongside the larger island. A single strip of concrete marked the private runway, two other planes parked beside a hangar. As they neared, a ferry boat came into focus. To ride from the airport to the main island? They sure were serious about security. Duarte had said it wasn't his secret to reveal. She thought of his father, a man who'd been overthrown in a violent coup. And his brothers, Carlos and Antonio, had a stake in this, as well. None of the Medina heirs had signed on for the royal life.

God, she missed the days when her job had been about providing valuable information to the public. It had been two years since she'd been in the trenches uncovering dirty politics and the nuances of complicated wars as opposed to shining a public flashlight on good people who had every right to their privacy.

The intercom system crackled a second before the pilot announced, "We're about to begin our descent. Please return to your seats and secure your lap belts. Thank you, and we hope you had a pleasant flight."

A glass-smooth landing later, she climbed on board the ferry that would transport them to the main island. Crisp sea air replaced the recycled oxygen in the jet cabin. Her camera bag slung over her shoulder, she recorded the images with her eyes for now. Duarte would call the shots on when she could snap photos. Her stomach knotted even though there wasn't a wave in sight, a perfect day for boating. A dolphin led the way, fin slicing through the water, then submerging again.

An osprey circled over its nest and herons picked their way through sea oats along the shore like a pictorial feature straight out of *National Geographic*. Until you looked closer and saw the guard tower, the security cameras tucked in trees.

A guard waited on the dock, a gun strapped within easy reach to protect the small crowd gathered to greet them. She recognized the man and woman from recent coverage in the media. "That's your youngest brother, Antonio, and his fiancée."

Duarte nodded.

The wedding he had mentioned made perfect sense now. She'd started the ball rolling digging up information about the shipping magnate and his waitress mistress. But then they'd fallen off the map. Apparently Alys Cortez hadn't shared everything she knew about the Medinas.

The brothers shared the same dark hair, although Antonio's was longer with a hint of curl. Duarte had a lean runner's build, whereas she would have pegged his brother as a former high school wrestler.

What sort of school experience would the young princes have had on a secluded island?

As the boat docked, she realized another couple waited with Tony and Shannon. Javier Cortez stood with a woman just behind him. They couldn't possibly have permitted his cousin Alys to stay after she betrayed them. Although they allowed a reporter into their midst...

Duarte touched the small of her back as they walked down the gangplank. "There's someone here to see you."

She looked closer as Javier stepped aside and revealed—

Jennifer?

Disbelief rocked the plank under Kate's feet. What was going on? She looked back at Duarte and he simply smiled as if it was nothing unusual to scoop her sister out of her protective home without consulting Kate. Not that Jennifer seemed to notice anything unusual about this whole bizarre day.

Jumping with excitement, her sister waved from the dock, wearing jeans, layered tank tops and a lightweight jacket. Her ponytail lifted by the wind, she could have been any college coed on vacation. Physically, she showed no signs of the special challenges she faced. But Kate was all too aware of her sister's vulnerability.

A vulnerability that hit home all the harder now that Kate realized how easily someone could steal Jennifer away without her knowing. How could she ever hope to go on a remote shoot without worrying? What if her editor had been the one to pull this stunt?

Kate loved Jennifer more than anyone in the world. But the balance of that love wavered between sibling and motherly affection. The maternal drive to protect Jennifer burned fiercely inside her.

And Duarte had stepped over a line. How dare he use his security people to just scoop up Jennifer? He was supposed to be protecting her.

Her lips pursed tight, Kate held her anger, for now. She didn't want to upset her sister with a scene.

Jennifer hugged her tight before stepping back smiling. "Katie, are you surprised? We get to visit after all. Isn't it beautiful? Can we go swimming even though it's January? It's not snowing, like at home."

Kate forced a smile onto her own face, as well. "It might be a bit cool for that even now. But we could go for walks on the beach. Hope you brought comfy shoes."

"Oh, they have everything for me. He—" she pointed to Javier "—said so when he picked me up at school. I got to fly on an airplane and they had my favorite movie with popcorn. All these nice people were waiting to meet me when I got here a few minutes before you. Have you met them?"

Shaking her head, Kate let Jennifer continue with the introductions, which saved her from having to say anything for a while. More specifically, it offered her the perfect diversion to avoid looking at Duarte until she could get her emotions under control and him alone.

On the surface this seemed like a thoughtful gesture, but he should have consulted her, damn it. Thinking of Jennifer going off with people she didn't know scared the hell out of Kate.

As for the supposedly great assisted-living facility, they never should have let Jennifer leave without calling her first.

So much for giving him the benefit of the doubt, assuming he could be an ordinary, everyday kind of guy. Duarte assumed his way was best.

No worries about joining the ranks of his three-month-rejects club. Because she would be walking out on Duarte Medina on their one-month anniversary.

Nine

Duarte wasn't sure what had upset Kate, but without question, she'd gone into deep-freeze mode after the ferry crossing. He'd known the discussion about her dad made her uncomfortable, but not like this. He'd hoped seeing her sister would trump everything else and make her happy. He'd been wrong, and he intended to find out why—after he'd seen his father.

Two vehicles waited, as he'd requested. A limousine would take the women to the main house and Duarte would use the Porsche Cayenne four-wheel drive to visit the island clinic with Tony.

Watching Jennifer finish her introductions, Duarte was struck by how much she looked like her sister. They shared the same general build and rich brown hair, the strong island sun emphasizing caramel-colored highlights. But most of all, he couldn't miss how much Jennifer adored her older sister. The love and protectiveness Kate displayed was clearly returned.

Bringing them together had been the right thing. And here on his father's island he could offer the sisters some of the pampering they had been denied.

Duarte turned to Kate. "Javier will take you both back to the house. Shannon will help you settle in while I go see my father with Tony. Anything you need, just ask."

He dropped a quick kiss on Kate's cheek, playing the attentive fiancé.

Jennifer quickly hooked arms with her sister. "Let me see the ring…"

Their voices drifted off and Duarte faced his brother alone for the first time since he'd stepped off the ferry. Tony's normally lighthearted ways were nowhere in sight today.

Duarte took the keys from his younger brother's extended hand. "Any change in his condition?"

"His fever is down and the breathing treatments help him rest more comfortably." Tony closed the car door, sitting in the passenger seat. "But the core problem with his liver hasn't been solved."

He turned the key and the Porsche SUV purred to life. "Has he considered a transplant?"

"That's a sticky subject for the old guy." Tony hooked his arm out the open window as they pulled away from the ferry. "For starters, he would have to go to the mainland. His doctors are of mixed opinion as to whether he's a good candidate."

"So we just wait around for him to die?" What had happened to their father, the fighter? "That doesn't seem right."

Enrique may have turned into a recluse, but he'd

rebuilt a minikingdom of his own here off the coast of Florida. Duarte guided the vehicle along the narrow paved road paralleling the shore.

When he'd first arrived here as a kid, the tropical jungle had given him the perfect haven. He would evade the guards and run until his heart felt like it would burst. Over time he'd realized the pain had more to do with losing his mother, with watching her murder. Then he'd begun martial arts training as well so he could go back to San Rinaldo one day. So he could take out the people responsible for his mother's death.

By the time he reached adulthood, he realized he would never have the revenge he'd craved as a child. His only vengeance came in not letting them win. He wouldn't be conquered.

He'd thought his father carried the same resolve. Duarte forced his attention back on the present and his brother's words.

"His health concerns are complicated by more than just the remote locale. There's the whole issue of finding a donor. Chances are greatly increased when the donor is of the same ethnicity."

"Which means we should be tested. Maybe one of us can donate a lobe," Duarte said without hesitation.

"Again, he says no. He insists that route poses too great a risk to us." Tony stared out over the ocean. While Duarte had used running to burn off his frustration, the youngest Medina brother had gravitated to the shore for swimming, surfing and later, sailing.

"He's stubborn as hell."

Tony turned back, his grin wry. "You're one to talk. I'm surprised you actually brought Kate Harper here. And that you gave her our mother's ring. You're not exactly the forgiving sort."

It wasn't Beatriz's wedding ring—Carlos had that—and in fact Duarte hadn't remembered her wearing that one as clearly as he recalled the ruby she'd worn on her other hand. As a child, he'd toyed with it while she told him stories of her own family. She'd been of royal descent, but her parents had been of modest means. She'd wanted her sons to value hard work and empathize with the people of San Rinaldo.

What would life have been like if she'd made it out of the country with them?

But she hadn't, and what-ifs wasted time. Her death must be weighing heavier on his mind because of his father's failing health. And now, he would see his father for what could be the last time.

The clinic—a one-story building, white stucco with a red tile roof—sported two wings, perched like a bird on the manicured lawn. One side held the offices for regular checkups, eye exams and dental visits. The other side was reserved for hospital beds, testing and surgeries.

Duarte parked the car in front and pocketed the keys. Guards nodded a welcome without relaxing their stance. They weren't Buckingham Palace-stiff, but their dedication to their mission couldn't be missed.

Electric doors slid open. A blast of cool, antiseptic air drifted out. The clinic was fully staffed with doctors and nurses on hand to see to the health concerns of the small legion that ran Enrique's island home. Most were from San Rinaldo or relatives of the refugees.

Tony pointed to the correct door, although Duarte would have known from the fresh pair of heavily armed sentinels. Bracing, he stepped inside the hospital room.

The former king hadn't requested any special accom-modations beyond privacy. There were no flowers or balloons or even cards to add color to the sterile space. The stark room held a simple chair, a rolling tray, a computer...

And a single bed.

Wearing paisley pajamas, Enrique Medina needed a shave. That alone told Duarte how ill the old man was.

He'd also lost weight since Duarte's last visit in May when he'd brought their half sister Eloisa over for her first trip to the island since she was a child. His father had been making a concerted effort to reconcile with his children.

A sigh rattled Enrique's chest and he adjusted the plastic tubes feeding oxygen into his nose. "Thank you for coming, *mi hijo*."

My son.

"Of course." He stepped deeper into the room. The old man had never been the hugging type. Duarte clapped him on the shoulder once. Damn, nothing but skin and bones. "Antonio says you're responding well to the treatment. When are you going to get a liver transplant?"

Scowling from one son to the other, Enrique said, "When did you become a nag like your brother?"

Tony spun on his heel. "I think I hear the guards calling me."

When the door closed, Duarte gave no quarter. "Still as stubborn as ever, I see, old man. I just didn't expect you to stop fighting."

"I'm still alive, am I not? My doctors wrote me off months ago." He waved a hand, veins bruised from IVs. "Enough about my health. I have no interest in discussing my every ache and ailment. I want to know more about your fiancée."

Duarte dropped into a chair. "Ah, so you held on long enough to meet her? Perhaps I should delay the introduction."

"If one of you promised a grandchild, you might get nine more months out of me."

"It's unfair to put your mortality on our shoulders."

"You are right," Enrique said, his calculating eyes still as sharp as ever in spite of his failing body. "What do you intend to do about it?"

Duarte weighed his next words. The old monarch passed on his sense of humor to Antonio and his intense drive to Carlos.

Duarte inherited his father's strategic abilities. Which told him exactly what he needed to say to get Enrique out of the hospital bed.

"You can meet Kate…when you get well enough to leave the clinic and come back to the house."

Kate had expected an amazing house. But nothing could have prepared her for the well-guarded opulence of the Medina mansion. Every *ooh* and *aah* from Jennifer as she caught her first glimpse reminded Kate of the awkward position Duarte had placed them in. Although she certainly didn't blame her sister.

Who wouldn't stare at the trees and the wildlife and the palatial residence? She and Jennifer had grown up in a small three-bedroom Cape Cod–style house outside Boston, comfortable in their second-story rooms. Kate had painted Jennifer's a bright yellow to go with photos she'd snapped of sunflowers and birds. She'd put a lot of effort into creating a space for her sister, the way a mother would have done. Jennifer had called the room her garden.

No wonder her sister was entranced by the botanical

explosion surrounding the Medina mansion. The place was the size of some hotels. Except she usually wasn't escorted to her hotel by a scowling head of security. Javier sat beside Shannon, eyeing Kate suspiciously the whole drive over.

The limousine slowed, easing past a towering marble fountain with a "welcome" pineapple on top—and wasn't that ironic in light of all those guards? Once the vehicle stopped, more uniformed security appeared from out of nowhere to open the limo.

Even a butler waited beside looming double doors.

Once inside, Kate couldn't hold back a gasp of her own. The cavernous circular hall sported gilded archways leading to open rooms. Two staircases stretched up either side, meeting in the middle. And she would bet good money that the Picasso on the wall wasn't a reproduction.

Shannon touched her elbow. "Everything will be taken up to the room."

"We don't have much." Kate passed her camera bag and Jennifer's backpack to the butler. "Duarte told me they—"

"—already have everything prepared. That's the Medina way," Shannon said, her words flavored with a light Texas twang. "Let's go straight through to the veranda. I'd like you to meet my son, Kolby."

Her footsteps echoing on the marble floor, Kate thought back to what she knew about Antonio Medina's fiancée and remembered the widowed Shannon had a three-year-old child from her first marriage, the boy she'd called Kolby.

Kate walked past what appeared to be a library. Books filled three walls, interspersed with windows and a sliding brass ladder. The smell of fresh citrus hung in the air, and not just because of the open windows. A tall potted orange tree nestled in one corner beneath a wide skylight. Mosaic tiles swirled outward on the floor, the ceiling filled with frescoes of globes and conquistadors. She pulled her eyes from the elaborate mural as they reached French doors leading out to a pool and seaside veranda.

A million-dollar view spread in front of her, and a towheaded little boy sprinted away from his sitter toward his mom. Shannon scooped up Kolby, the future princess completely natural and informal with her son.

Kate decided then and there that she liked the woman.

Shuffling Kolby to her hip, Shannon turned to Jennifer. "What would you like to do today?"

"What do I get to pick from?" Jennifer spun on her tennis shoes. "Are you sure it's too cold to go swimming in the ocean?"

Kate's heart warmed at Shannon's obvious ease with Jennifer.

"You could take a dip in the pool out here. It's heated." Shannon patted her son's back as he drooped against her, eyes lolling. "There's also a movie theater with anything you want to see. They've added a spa with pedicures and manicures even recently."

Jennifer clapped her hands. "Yes, that's what I want, painted toenails and no snow boots."

Laughing, Shannon set her groggy son on a lounger and walked to the drink bar. "You're a kindred spirit."

"What does that mean?" Jennifer asked.

Shannon poured servings of lemonade—fresh squeezed, no doubt. "We're sister spirits." She passed crystal goblets to each of them. Her eyes were curious behind retro black glasses. "I live to have my feet massaged."

"And when Katie marries Artie—" Jennifer's brown eyes lit with excitement as she clutched her drink "—we'll be sisters for real since you're marrying his brother."

Shannon spewed her sip. "Artie?"

Stifling a smile, Kate set aside her lemonade. "He prefers to be called Duarte."

Seeing how quickly Jennifer accepted these people into her heart sent a trickle of unease down Kate's spine. This was just the kind of thing she'd wanted to avoid. Explaining the breakup would have been difficult enough before. But now? It would be far more upsetting. Her frustration with Duarte grew.

Jennifer hooked arms with her sister. "I know you're the one who is going to marry Artie—uh, Duarte. But I already feel like a princess."

Duarte had done his best to leave his princely roots behind and lead his own life. But there was no escaping the Medina mantle here. Even the "informal" dinner at this place was outside the norm, something he realized more so when seeing the all-glass dining area through other people's eyes. Shannon's young son loved the room best since he said it was like eating in a jungle with trees visible through three walls and the ceiling.

Throughout the meal, Kate had stayed silent for the most part, only answering questions when directly asked. He wanted to tell himself she was simply tired. But now, watching her charge through her bedroom taking inventory of her surroundings and setting up her computer, she brimmed with frustrated energy. Her dress whipped around her leather knee boots.

No more waiting. He had to know what had set her off. "Tell me."

"Tell you what?" She spun away from the canopy bed, anger shooting icicles from her eyes. "It's helpful to a person when you elaborate rather than bark out one- and two-word orders."

He was completely clueless as to what pissed her off and that concerned him more than anything. He should at least have some idea. "Explain to me what has made you angry, and don't bother denying that you're upset."

"Oh, believe me." She sauntered closer, stopping by her camera case resting on a chaise at the end of her bed. "I wasn't planning to deny a thing. I was simply waiting for a private moment alone with you."

"Then let's have it."

She jabbed him in the chest, the kimono sleeves of her dress whispering against him. "You had no right to interfere in my life by bringing Jennifer here."

What the hell? Her accusation blindsided him. "I thought seeing your sister would make you happy."

"Do you have any idea how hard it was to get her into that facility, a place that fits her needs but also makes her happy?" Her words hissed through clenched teeth as she obviously tried to keep her voice down. "What if they give someone else her spot?"

That, he could fix. "I will make sure it doesn't happen."

"Argh!" She growled her frustration. "You can't just take over like that. You're not responsible for her. You have no say in her life. And while we're on that subject, how did you even arrange for her to leave? Good God, maybe I should move her anyway if security is that lax in the center. I'm shelling out a small fortune for Jennifer to live there. What if someone had kidnapped her?"

All right, he could see her point somewhat, even if he didn't agree. "I told you before. I had round-the-clock guards watching her *and* the facility—" he saw her jaw tighten and added "—which is quite nice by the way, like a boarding school. You've done an admirable job for your sister."

And she'd done it all alone without her father's help. That kind of pressure could explain her over-the-top reaction.

"I searched long and hard to find a place where she could live given how much I have to travel." Her chest heaved and her cheeks pinked with her rising emotions. "It wasn't easy and now you've jeopardized that. I simply can't let it pass that they released her to you without even consulting me."

Now he was starting to get pissed off himself. He'd been thinking of her and he wasn't accustomed to explaining himself to people. "I'm not a random stranger claiming a connection. It's well documented and, thanks to your job, highly publicized that I'm your fiancé. My name is known at that facility whether you like it or not and Javier was acting on my authority. We have the space for Jennifer here, as well as the staff on hand for anything she needs. In case you didn't notice, she's very happy with the arrangement."

"Of course she's happy. And that's going to make it all the tougher when we have to go back to our everyday, middle-class life. I can't afford—" she gestured around her wildly, her eyes lingering on a framed Esteban March battle painting "—all of this. I don't want her getting attached to the lifestyle."

Then it became clear. He stroked down her arm,

ready to entice her anger away in the canopy bed. "*You* don't want to get attached."

She dodged his touch. "You'll be out of my life in about three weeks. You've only been *in* my life less than a week. Be honest, you don't want a real relationship with me any more than I want to be a part of your crazy world. This needs to stop before someone gets hurt. We have to go back to our original arrangement."

Like hell. Anger kicked around inside him as hard as her words in his brain, her insistence that she didn't want to be involved with the Medina mess. "Do you think backing off will erase what happened last night and again today? Will you be able to forget? Because I damn well can't."

He could see those same memories scrolling across her mind.

Her gaze locked on him as firmly as his stayed on her. Moonlight played with hints of the caramel-colored highlights in her brown hair, glinted off the deepening blue of her eyes. He wanted her so much he went rock hard in a flash.

His life would be so much simpler without this attraction.

"Duarte, I haven't forgotten a second," she whispered.

Heat flared in her eyes as hot as the fire licking through his veins and he knew he wouldn't trade a second of the connection with Kate. He knew she couldn't ignore this any more than he could. Duarte started across the room just as Kate joined him, mouths meeting, passion exploding.

They fell back onto the canopy bed.

Ten

Duarte tucked Kate under him on the canopy bed, her frenetic kisses tapping into all the frustration burning his insides. Static lifted strands of her hair toward him, crackling off his face in an echo of the charged need snapping through him.

After their fight tonight, he hadn't expected another chance to be with her. Her seductive wriggle he now knew encouraged him to press his thigh closer. She sighed, urging him on with her gasps and fingers digging deeper into his back.

Their legs tangled in the spread. Without moving his mouth from hers, he wadded the coverlet and flung it on the floor. He tunneled his hand under the hem of her dress. The cool sheets slithered underneath them, the high thread count nowhere near as silky as her skin.

"Clothes," she whispered between nips, "we have too many."

He knew an invitation when he heard one.

"Let me help you with that."

Drawing his mouth from hers, he nuzzled down her body until he reached her long legs. She'd driven him crazy all day long with the killer boots. As he eased down one knee-high leather boot, he kissed along her calf, her skin creamy and soft. Her breathy moan, the impatient grapple of her hands on his shoulders encouraged him. He tugged the other boot down and sent it to the floor with a resounding thump.

Kate curled her toes, wriggling the painted white tips in a delicious stretch that called his fingers to her delicate arches. Stretching to the side, she switched on the bedside lamp.

He stroked along her arm and gathered her against him again. "You don't shy away from the light. That's a total turn-on."

She hooked a leg over his hip. "You're such a *guy*."

"Obviously." His erection throbbed between them.

Her eyes narrowed with purpose. "Lie back."

"We'll get there." He slanted his mouth over hers.

She flattened her palm against his chest. "I said for you to lie back." Determination resonated from her words as sure as the unremitting surf rolling outside the open veranda doors. "You give a lot of orders. I think it's time for someone to take charge of you."

"Are you challenging me to a power struggle?"

"I'm daring you to give your body over to me. Or does the prince always have to be in control?"

Her question hinted at their argument earlier, and damned if he would let this moment be derailed. His hand glided up to cradle her breast. "What do you have in mind?"

"No, no." She shook her head slowly, tousled hair

a sexy cloud of disarray around her face. "If I spell everything out, you're not taking much of a risk."

Her meaning crystallized in his mind. "So I trust you a little and you trust me a little?"

"You first," she said, the mix of vixen and vulnerability winning him over.

He whipped his shirt off, reclined back. And waited.

Standing at the foot of the bed, she bunched the hem of her dress in her hands, inch by inch exposing her thighs to his hungry gaze. Then showing her cranberry-red panties and bra he'd peeled from her earlier in the airplane.

Her dress covered her face for an instant before she flung it aside. The salty sea air through the French doors fluttered the canopy overhead and her breasts beaded visibly against the satin bra. His hands fisted in the sheets as he resisted the urge to haul her against him right then and there. She shook her hair from her face, flicking it over her shoulders.

"Your turn," she demanded.

God, she was hot and turned him inside out in a way no other woman had. He tugged his pants and boxers off, ready to cut short this game of dare or strip poker or whatever she wanted to call it.

She quirked a brow then reached for the center clasp—he swallowed hard—to unfasten her bra. Red satin fell away and he couldn't resist. He arched off the bed toward her.

Shaking her head, she covered her breasts and backed up. He reclined again, his arms behind his head. She lowered her hands and hooked her thumbs in her panties. A slow shimmy later, she kicked aside the underwear.

Her eyes blazed bold and determined as she knelt on

the bed. Crawling up the mattress, she climbed toward him. He slid his hands from behind his head, flattened along the sheets, but didn't touch her, not yet. The intensity in her eyes said she wanted to play this out a while longer. He didn't delude himself that this would magically fix their argument, and they might be better served talking.

But damned if he could find the words or will to stop her.

She fanned her fingers over his chest. A primitive growl rumbled free ahead of his thoughts. She dipped her head and flicked her tongue over his flat nipple. Again. She devoted every bit as much attention to him as he'd enjoyed lavishing on her beautiful body earlier in the plane. Drawing circles down his stomach, she scratched lightly down and down. His abs contracted under her touch.

Lower still she traced just beside his arousal until his teeth clenched. Then her cool hand curled around him and stroked, deliberately, continuing until his eyes slammed shut and his senses narrowed to just the glide of her touch. The caress of her thumb. The warmth of her mouth.

Dots specked behind his eyelids, the roar in his ears rivaling the crash of waves. His jaw clamped tight as he held back his release, fought the urge to move.

"Kate…" he hissed between clenched teeth.

Shifting, she stretched upward again, her lips leading the way as she kissed, licked, nipped until she reached his face.

Once he opened his eyes, she stared down at him. "Where do you keep the birth control?"

His desire-steamed brain raced to keep pace. "In my

wallet. I would reach for it, but someone told me not to move. Do you mind?"

With a fluid stretch over the side, she plucked his wallet from his pants and pulled out a condom. Flipping the packet between her fingers, she smiled at him with such a wicked glint in her now-near-purplish-blue eyes that he knew she wasn't through with her control game. Not by a long shot. She smoothed the condom down and took him inside her with such sweet torturous precision he almost came undone.

The restraints snapped and his hands shot up to cup her breasts. She pushed into his palms, tips harder and tighter than ever before. Her instant response to his touch sent a rush of possessiveness through him.

She cradled his face as she rocked her hips. "I would love to capture your expression on film."

"There I have to draw the line." He finger-combed her hair, bringing her mouth to his as he thrust again and again.

"I have to agree," she murmured against his lips, eyes wide, intimate as they watched, touched, even talked, both completely into each other and the moment. "As much as I would love to take your picture right now, the last thing we need is someone hacking into my computer and finding naked photos of you."

She'd surprised him there. But then he should be used to the way she lobbed bombshells his way. "You want to take risqué pictures of me?"

"I beg your pardon? I had something more artistic in mind." She ground her hips against his as she continued to whisper her fantasy. "But yes, you would be totally, gloriously, naked."

He throbbed inside the satiny clasp of her body. While he couldn't imagine himself pulling some pretty-boy naked modeling session even for Kate, he absolutely enjoyed hearing her fantasize. "Artistic how?"

"You're a mesmerizing man. The way light plays across the cut of your muscles in your arms, the six-pack ridges. Everything about you is stark angles. And shadows. The things I see when I look in your eyes..."

"Enough." He kissed her hard to break off her words, uncomfortable with the turn her scenario had taken. To hell with giving over control. He rolled her to her back and she didn't protest.

In a flash, she hooked her legs around his waist and took charge of her pleasure—of theirs—all over again. And it was every bit as combustible as before. The glide of sweat-slicked skin against skin, the scent of her with him lingering in the air. He couldn't get enough of her. Even as they thrust toward completion, he knew the sex between them would always be thus.

And it hadn't brought them any closer to resolving their argument.

A week later, Kate snapped a photo of Jennifer lounging in a hammock strung between two palm trees. Jennifer tucked in one earbud for her new iPod, boy-band music drifting from the other loose earpiece.

Click. Click.

Kate had photos galore, much to Harold Hough's delight, although in his emails he kept pressing for one of the king. She could answer honestly that she hadn't seen him. The monarch was still in the hospital. She hadn't been allowed access.

Focusing on her favorite Canon camera and her job rather than her confusing relationship with Duarte, Kate swung the lens toward her next subject. Antonio straddled a paddleboard in the shallow tides with little

Kolby in front of him, both of them wearing wet suits for the cooler waters. *Click. Click.*

These photos would be her wedding gifts to Shannon and Tony. Some pictures she considered off-limits to Harold Hough, the *Intruder* and the public in general. During the past week, she'd found herself more protective of the images than even Duarte. These people had welcomed her into their lives and they trusted her to represent them fairly in the media. She'd learned there were some moral lines she refused to cross, even for her sister.

Lifting the camera, she went back to work on images for her gift to the bride and groom. Two large dogs loped in the surf, the king's trained Rhodesian Ridgebacks named Benito and Diablo. *Click.* The dogs might look scary but they were pussycats around the little boy.

A strange squeeze wrapped around Kate's heart as she took a close-up of the child and his soon-to-be dad in matching wet suits. The towheaded little boy sported white zinc oxide on his nose and a big grin on his face.

Lowering her camera, she wondered how Duarte would act with his children someday. He wasn't the lighthearted playmate sort like Tony, but she'd seen his gentle patience and understanding with Jennifer over the past week. Her heart went tight again.

Don't think.

Duarte wore jeans and a lightweight pullover, wind threading in off the ocean and playing with his hair the way she longed to. From a distance he may have appeared casual, lounging back against a tree. But through her lens, Kate saw the iPhone in his hand and he sure wasn't playing music. His brow furrowed, he seemed intent on business.

Their week together had been guarded to say the least. While the king stayed isolated in the hospital, they'd settled into an unspoken standoff, participating in five-star family dinners. Smiling at movie nights in the home theater. Sailing. Swimming. Even going to the gym with a stationary bike for her to work off all the meals while Duarte completed a martial arts workout looking like sex personified.

Most would have considered the week a dream vacation.

Except Duarte hadn't apologized for his autocratic move in bringing Jennifer to the island without consulting her. And she simply couldn't tell him never mind, it didn't matter. Because it *was* important.

Although, she didn't understand why she felt so compelled to make her point. They would be out of each other's lives in another two weeks or so when she took the photos of Tony and Shannon's wedding. She should just enjoy the sex and let the deeper issues float away like palmetto fronds on the waves.

And the sex was most definitely enjoyable.

While their days together might be tension packed, the nights were passion filled. In her bed or his, they never planned ahead but somehow found their way into each other's arms by midnight, staying together until sunrise.

Pictures. Right. She'd forgotten.

Click, click, click. She captured Duarte in photos just for her personal collection when she left the island. After all, she would probably need proof for herself that it all happened in the first place. Every moment here felt surreal, a dream life she'd never been meant to live.

She shifted the lens.

Shannon sat cross-legged on a beach blanket with

a basket, arranging a picnic lunch. "Okay, y'all," she drawled, nudging her glasses in place, "we have roasted turkey and cheese with apricot-fig chutney on a baguette, spinach salad with champagne vinaigrette, and fresh fruit tarts for dessert. And for Kolby…" She pulled out what appeared to be lunch meat rolled in tortillas. Her blonde ponytail swished in the wind as she called out to her son and future husband. *Click. Click.* "Caterpillars and snakes."

Jennifer swung a leg over the side of the hammock and toe-tapped it into motion, rocking gently. "Tortillas as snakes? You're a fun mom, Shannon."

The young mother placed the deli rollups on a Thomas the Tank Engine plate. "Anything to make mealtime an adventure rather than a battle."

Swiping moisture off the lens, Kate refocused on her sister. "This reminds me of home in the summer, with picnics by the shore."

Before life had turned vastly complicated.

Jennifer adjusted her pink polka-dot visor. "Except it's January. I could get used to no snow." Her younger sister glanced at Duarte leaning against the tree at her feet. "Why did you wanna live somewhere so different from here? This is perfect."

"Not that different." He looked over patiently, tucking away his iPhone in a waterproof backpack. "Living on Martha's Vineyard reminds me of the parts of home that meant most to me, the rocky shore, the sailboats."

Something in his voice told Kate by "home" he meant San Rinaldo, not this island. For Duarte growing up, the luxury here must have seemed a poor substitute for all he'd lost. The sun dimmed behind a cloud.

Slipping from the hammock to stand beside Duarte, Jennifer pulled out her earbud and wrapped the cord around the iPod. "And when your toes get too cold, you can simply visit one of your other resorts."

"Like your sister travels with her job."

Kate's finger twitched on the next shot.

Her sister scrunched her nose. "Yeah, but the postcards aren't as fun anymore." Jennifer's face cleared. "I still have the one she sent me from an airport in Paris when she was on her way to somewhere else. I don't remember where, but the postcard has the Eiffel Tower on it. Cool, huh?"

"Very cool, Jennifer."

"Hey." Shannon smiled from the blanket. "Duarte and Kate can fly you to the Eiffel Tower in their family jet."

Kate gasped and bit her tongue hard to keep from snapping back while Jennifer chattered excitedly about the possibility of such a trip. Shannon had no way of knowing she'd raised Jennifer's hopes for nothing. Kate nearly staggered under the weight of her deception. The future Medina bride had no idea this whole engagement was a farce. Kate hadn't foreseen how many people would be affected—would be hurt—by this charade.

Including herself.

What a time to realize she didn't want this to end in two weeks. She wasn't sure what the future held, but how amazing it would have been to date Duarte for real, let a real relationship follow its course. Her thumb went to the engagement ring, turning the stone round and round. Her camera slid from her slack grip to thud against the sand.

Oh, God. She dropped to her knees and dusted the camera frantically. She didn't have the money to replace her equipment. She knew better than to get caught up in some fairy-tale life that included flights to Paris and inherited family jewels, for crying out loud. What was the matter with her?

A shadow stretched beside her a second before Duarte knelt near her, offering her lens cloth. "Need this?"

"Thank you." She felt so confused. He'd given her nothing more than himself this week, making his body delectably available to her increasing demands, but never letting her have a glimpse of the heart within.

How long could they play this sensual teasing game before they hurt too many people to count?

"You miss it," he said. "The travel with your old job, before *Intruder* days of star chasing."

Ah. The least of her troubles right now. But then, Duarte had no idea he'd touched her heart in a way she could never seem to penetrate his.

Wary of being overheard, she checked on the rest of their party and found they'd moved away from the blanket, involved in setting up an elaborate new sunshade tent for Kolby's lunch. She looked back at Duarte quickly.

"My sister needs continuity," she responded and evaded his question. "This is the only way I can earn a living that provides for her."

"Perhaps there are different ways to find continuity than living in one particular place."

Did the man learn nothing? There he went again, presuming to handle Jennifer's life for her. Frustration from the past week boiled to life again. "Spoken like a man who lives in hotels, a man scared of having a real home."

A real connection, damn it.

They stared at each other in a standoff that had become all too common over the past seven days. Except with her heart aching she wondered how she could simply indulge in heated, no-strings sex with him tonight when they had failed to find common ground in every other arena of their lives.

Swallowing back a lump in her throat, she stood. "I should go and upload these photos. My editor's expecting an update and I would hate to miss a deadline."

Duarte clasped her arm, his eyes broadcasting his intent to press her for more…when a Jeep roared in the distance, rumbling across the sandy beach toward them. As the vehicle drove closer, Javier Cortez came into sight behind the wheel. The four-wheel drive skidded to a stop, spewing sand from the tires.

The head of security grabbed the roll bar and swung to the ground. "Duarte, I wanted to tell you in person."

Shannon shot to her feet, gasping. "Is it their father? Is he…?"

Tony rushed up the shore, his board under one arm, his other hand holding tight to little Kolby. "Javier?"

Cortez held a hand up. "Calm down, everyone. It's good news that I thought you should hear face-to-face. The king has recovered enough to be released from the hospital. He will be home by the end of the day."

The weight on Kate's shoulders increased as she thought of fooling yet another person with the fake engagement. This time, they added an old man in frail health to the list of people who would be hurt. And right now, she worried less about how she would be able to forgive Duarte and more about how she would ever forgive herself.

Eleven

His father was home.

Duarte had been as stunned as everyone else by Enrique's surge of energy. But the old man made it clear. He wanted to meet Kate.

Guiding her down the hall toward the wing housing his father's quarters, Duarte kept his hand on her back to steer her through the winding corridors. He barely registered the familiar antique wooden benches tucked here, a strategic table and guard posted there, too preoccupied with the introduction to come.

What the hell was up with the edginess? He'd planned this from the start, to bring her along to appease the old man. They'd made a business proposition. So why did the whole thing suddenly feel off?

Because they'd clearly gone from business to personal in the past week and that rocked him to the core. He wanted more. Over the past weeks, she'd surprised him in ways he never could have foreseen. Like how she'd left her camera behind for this meeting with the king.

She'd told him that she planned to limit her photos of the king to the old man's appearance at Tony's wedding. For that matter, Duarte had been surprised at how few pictures she opted to send to the *Intruder* overall. Since the world was getting a steady flow of photos, news outlets ran those and weren't searching as hard for others. The interest hadn't gone away, but Javier's security team back home wasn't peeling as many reporters off the fences.

Now, entering the monarch's private suites, Duarte tried to focus on the present. While the mansion sported a small fortune in works of art by Spanish masters, Enrique saved his Salvador Dali collection for himself, a trio of the surrealist's "soft watches" melting over landscapes.

The old guy had become more obsessed with history after his had been stolen from him.

Cradling his antique Breguet pocket watch, Enrique waited in his bed, sitting on top of the cover, wearing a heavy blue robe and years of worries. His father's two Rhodesian Ridgebacks lounged on the floor at the foot of the bed. Brown, leggy and large, the dogs provided protection as well as companionship. Kate leaned down to pet Benito, the dogs accepting her because she was with Duarte.

Frail and pasty, Enrique appeared to be sleeping. Then his eyes snapped open with a sharp gleam in his gaze.

"Father." Duarte kept his hand planted on the small of her back. "This is Kate."

Enrique tucked his watch into his robe pocket and stayed silent, his coal-dark eyes assessing Kate. Duarte slid his arm farther around her, bringing her closer to his side. "Father?"

Kate rested a hand on his softly and stepped forward, facing the old man head-on and bold as always. "I'm glad you're well enough to return home, sir."

Still, his father didn't speak and Duarte began to wonder if Enrique had taken a turn for the worse. Was his once-sharp mind now failing, as well?

Kate stepped closer, magnificent in her unfailing confidence. "Do you mind if I sit?"

Still staring intently, Enrique motioned to the leather armchair beside his bed.

Sinking onto the seat, Kate perched a bit more formally than normal, her legs tucked demurely to the side. But other than that, she showed no sign of nerves in meeting the deposed king.

She pointed toward the framed painting closest to his bed. "I've always been a fan of Dali's melting watch works."

"You've studied the Masters?"

"I took art history classes in college along with my journalism degree. I can't paint or draw to save my soul, but I like to think I capture natural art and tell a story with my lens."

"I've seen some of your earlier photographs in our security file on you. You have an artist's eye."

She didn't even wince over the background check, something his father appeared to have noticed, too.

Pushing against the mattress, Enrique sat up straighter. "You're not upset that I had you investigated?"

"I investigated your family. It only seems fair you should have the same freedom."

Enrique laughed, rumbly but genuine. "I like the way you think, Kate Harper." He lifted her hand and eyed the ring, thumbing the top of the ruby once before nodding. "A good fit."

With that succinct endorsement, his father leaned back on the pillow, his eyes sliding closed again.

That was it? Duarte had expected…something more. Digs for specifics on a wedding date. Hints for grandchildren. Even a crack at her profession, and that made him wonder if perhaps there'd been something to Javier's accusation that he'd chosen Kate to jab back at the old man, after all.

If so, the joke was soundly on Duarte, because seeing Kate reach out to his father stirred a deeper sense of family than Duarte had ever felt before. Watching her in this setting finally pounded home what had been going on for weeks without him even noticing. Kate was more a part of his world than he was. She was a seamless fit in a high-stress environment, a strong but calming influence on the people around her, an intelligent and quick-witted woman who knew her mind and took care of her own.

What a kick in the ass to realize Kate was right about his lack of commitment to even a house, much less a relationship. He'd always prided himself on being a man of decisive action, yet when it had come to Kate, he'd been living in limbo—granted, a sex-saturated limbo—but limbo all the same.

Time to take action. He had about two weeks until his brother's wedding and he needed to utilize every second to persuade Kate to stay in his life after the thirty-day deadline.

Whatever the cost.

Gasping, Kate bolted upright in her bed. Alone.

Her heart pounding out of her chest, she searched the

room for him…but no luck. She'd fallen asleep in his arms, slipping into a nightmare where she'd melted away like a Dali watch, sliding from the ledge of Duarte's resort on Martha's Vineyard.

Sliding away from him.

She scraped her hair back from her face, the sheets slithering over her bare skin. The scent of his aftershave clung to the linens as surely as he lingered in her memories. He'd been so intense, so thorough tonight.

Stretching, her arm bumped something on the pillow. She jolted back and switched on the Tiffany lamp. A wrapped present waited in the cradle left by the imprint of his head. She clamped a hand to her mouth at the flat twelve-by-twelve package, a maroon box with a gold bow and no card. Not that she needed a card to know. Receiving a gift was different from the jewels and clothes he'd given her as part of the public charade. This was a private moment.

Why hadn't he stayed to see her reaction? Could he be as unsure as she was about where and how to proceed next?

Her stomach churned with excitement and fear. Maybe she was working herself up for nothing. Wouldn't she feel foolish if the present turned out to be a new gown to wear to the wedding? Or some other accoutrement to play out their fake engagement?

Her heart squeezed tight at the memory of meeting Enrique, a delightful old man who took her at face value and reeled her right in. Guilt had niggled at her ever since deceiving him—a warm and wonderful father figure to a woman so sorely lacking in that department. She hated to think about all the lies yet to come.

But there was only one way to find out what the box held. She swept the gift from the pillow, heavier than she'd expected. Curiosity overcame her fear and she tore off the crisp gold bow, then the thick maroon paper. Lifting the lid from the box, she found...

A small framed black-and-white photo—oh, God, an Ansel Adams of a moonrise over icy mountain peaks. Her hand shook as her fingers hovered over the image. He'd remembered. Just one conversation about her favorite photographer and he'd committed it to memory, choosing this gift with her preferences in mind.

Yes, he'd overstepped in spiriting Jennifer away, but he was obviously trying to woo her. And not with something generic that could have been ordered for any interchangeable woman.

Kate set the gift aside reverently and swept the covers away. She had to find him, to thank him, to see if she was reading too much into one gift. She stepped into the closet—good heavens, Duarte and his family had closet space to spare. She grabbed for the first pair of jeans and a pullover. Dressing on her way out of the room, she scanned the sitting area for Duarte.

The balcony door stood open.

Different from the wrought-iron railing she'd seen on the other side of the house when she'd arrived, this terrace sported a waist-high, white stucco wall with potted cacti and hanging ferns. In her time on the island, she'd realized the house had four large wings of private quarters, one for the king and three for his sons. Here, wide stone steps led down toward the beach, yellow moon and stars reflecting off the dark stretch of ocean.

She scanned and didn't see anything other than rolling waves and a small cluster of palm trees. As she turned away, a squeak stopped her short. She pivoted back and peered closer into the dark.

Moonlight peeked through the clouds long enough to stream over a hammock strung between two towering trees. The ghostly white light reminded her of the gorgeous photograph he'd given her. Duarte lounged with one leg draped off the side, swinging slowly. She couldn't think of when she'd seen him so unguarded.

Hand dragging along the wall, she raced down the steps. A chilly breeze off the water lifted her hair, night temperature dipping. The squeak slowed and she realized he must have heard her.

As she neared, her eyes adjusted to the dark. Duarte wore the same silky ninja workout clothes as the night they'd met. Looking closer, she saw a hint of perspiration still clung to his brow. He must have gone to the home gym after she'd fallen asleep. She was increasingly realizing he channeled martial arts moments to vent pent-up frustration.

Breathless—from the sight of him more than the jog—she leaned against the palm tree. "Thank you for the gift."

"You're welcome," he said softly, extending an arm for her to join him on the hammock.

Almost afraid to hope he might be reaching out to her on an even deeper level, she took his hand.

"It's such a perfect choice," she said as she settled against his warmth, the hammock jolting, rocking, finally steadying. "An Ansel Adams gift? Very nice."

"Any Joe with a big bank balance could have done that."

"But not just any Joe would have remembered what I named my cat." She brushed a kiss along his bristly jaw. "I can't wait to find just the right place to hang it."

Back at her apartment? Every time she looked at it,

she would be reminded of him. The air grew heavier as she breathed in the salt-tinged wind.

His arm under her shoulders, he fit her closer against him. "I'm glad you're happy."

It was one thing to talk in the course of a day or even in the aftermath of sex, but cuddling quietly in the moonlight was somehow more…intimate.

Furthermore, was she happy? At the moment, yes. But so much rode on the outcome of this month. She still feared disappointing so many people with a failed engagement.

"You're not what I expected, you know." She traced the V-neckline of his jacket. "But then that's my fault. It was easier to paint you as the arrogant rich prince. You try so hard, even when you screw up."

"Such as bringing Jennifer here without asking you." His deep voice rumbled over her hair, his chin resting on her head.

"Bonus points for admitting you were wrong." She stroked her toes over his bare feet beside hers.

"I *am* sorry for not consulting you before bringing Jennifer to the island."

She shifted to look up at him. "Did that apology hurt coming up?"

"I beg your pardon?"

Laughing, she swatted his chest. "I bet you've never begged for anything in your life. You're too proud."

"You would be wrong," he said so softly she almost missed the words. Then he squeezed her hand lightly. "I would give you an Ansel Adams gallery if you wish."

"Thank you, truly." She stretched to kiss him, just a closemouthed moment to linger and languish in the rightness of touching him. "But no need to go overboard.

The clothes, private planes, guards—I have to admit to feeling a little overwhelmed."

"You? Overwhelmed?" He sounded genuinely surprised. "I've only known one woman as bold as you."

For the first time that she could recall, he'd offered up a piece of personal information about himself. Another sign that he was trying to make amends? Get closer?

Her heart pounded so hard she wondered if he could feel it against his side. Was there a hidden, lost love in his past? "Who was the other woman?" she asked carefully. "The one as bold as I am?"

His heart beat so hard she *could* feel it under her palm. She waited, wondering if she'd misread his slip. And how would she feel if he suddenly revealed he'd been in love with someone else?

Finally, he answered, "My mother."

Everything inside her went still. Her senses pulled tightly into the world around her. The pulsing of her blood through her veins synched with the tide's gush and retreat. The palms overhead rustled as heavily as Duarte's breaths.

Kate stroked his chest lightly. "I would like to hear more about her."

"I would like to tell you…Carlos and I used to talk about her, verifying that our memories weren't becoming faulty with time. It's so easy for some moments to overtake others."

"The little things can be special."

"Actually, I'm talking about the bigger events." He paused, his neck moving against her in a long swallow. "Like the night she died."

She held her breath, terrified of saying something wrong. She'd covered dangerous and tragic situations in her job, back in the beginning, but she'd been seeing it all through a lens, as an observer. Her heart had ached for those suffering, but it was nothing compared to the wrenching pain of envisioning Duarte as a young boy living out one of those events.

"Kate? The fierce way my mother protected us reminds me of how you take care of Jennifer. I know you would lay down your life for her."

And he was right. But dear God, no woman should ever have to pay the price his mother had to look after her children. She closed her eyes to hold back the burning tears as she listened to Duarte.

"That night when the rebels caught us…" His chest pumped harder. "Carlos whispered for me to cover Antonio and he would look after our mother. When you said you couldn't imagine me ever begging…" He cleared his throat and continued, "I begged for my mother's life. I begged, but they shot her anyway. They shot Carlos because he tried to protect her…"

His voice cracked.

Her throat closed up with emotions, and now it wasn't a matter of searching for the right words because she couldn't speak at all. He'd planted an image so heartbreaking into her mind, it shattered her ability to reason. She just held him tighter.

"Once our mother died," he continued, his slight accent thickening with emotion, "time became a blur. I still can't remember how Antonio and I got away unscathed. Later I was told more of our father's guards arrived. After we left San Rinaldo, we spent a while in Argentina until we were reunited with our father."

Shivering more from the picture he painted than the cool night wind, she pushed words up and out. "Who was there to console you?"

He waved her question aside. "Once my father

arrived, we stayed long enough to establish rumors we'd relocated there. Then we left."

His sparse retelling left holes in the story, but regardless, it sounded as if there hadn't been much time for him to grieve such a huge loss. And to see his oldest brother shot, as well? That hadn't appeared in any news reports about the Medina family. What other horrifying details had they managed to keep secret?

Shadows cast by the trees and clouds grew murkier, dangerous. "It's no wonder that your father became obsessed with security and keeping his sons safe."

"And yet, he risked trips to the mainland those first couple years we were here."

"Your father left the island?" Where was Duarte going with this revelation? She had no idea, but she did know he never did anything without a purpose.

And she'd been so hungry for a peek inside his heart and his past for clues as to what made this man tick. She would be glad for whatever he cared to share tonight.

"My father had developed a relationship with another woman," he said, his voice flat and unemotional, overly so.

What he said merged with what she knew from covering his family. "You're talking about your half sister's mother." Kate knew the details, like the age of Enrique's daughter. Eloisa had been born less than two years after the coup in San Rinaldo. That affair had to have been tough for three boys still grieving the loss of their mother. "How did they meet?"

"Carlos's recovery from his gunshot wounds was lengthy. Between our time in Argentina and relocating here, Carlos had a setback. Our father met a nurse at the hospital." The muscles in Duarte's chest contracted. "He found distraction from his grief."

So much more made sense, like why Duarte and his brothers had little contact with their father. "His relationship with the nurse created a rift between you and your father."

It was easy to empathize with either side—a devastated man seeking comfort for an immeasurable loss. A boy resentful that his father had sought that comfort during such a confusing time of grief.

"You probably wonder why I'm telling you this."

She weighed the risks and figured the time had come to step out on an emotional ledge. "We've been naked together. While being with you is amazing, I would like to think we have more going for us than that."

"You've mentioned my numerous short relationships."

She hated the pinch of jealousy. "Your point?"

"I've had sex, but I don't have much experience with building relationships. Not with my family. Not with women. I've been told I'm an emotionless bastard."

"Emotionless? Good God, Duarte," she exclaimed, shifting over him, hammock lurching much like her feelings, "you're anything but detached. You're one of the most intense people I've ever met. Sure you don't crack a bunch of jokes and get teary eyed at commercials, but I see how deeply you feel things."

He silenced her with a finger to her mouth. "You're misunderstanding. I'm telling you I want more than just your body."

Her stomach bumped against her heart. Could he really mean...

"But, Kate, I can't be sure I have the follow-through. Given my history, I'm a risk to say the least."

Hearing this proud man lay himself bare before her this way tugged at her heart, already tender from images of a hurting young boy. She thought of the considerate gift, left on her pillow rather than presented in person. Could he be every bit as unsettled by their relationship as she was? He acted so confident, so in control.

Unease whispered over her like the night wind blowing in off the ocean. He'd said a relationship with him was a risk and she was just beginning to realize how much she had to lose—a chance with Duarte, a chance at his heart.

So much had changed so fast for both of them. If he was every bit as confused and stunned by the feelings erupting between them, perhaps the best answer would be a careful approach.

"Duarte," she whispered against his mouth, "how about we take it one day at a time until Tony and Shannon's wedding?"

Shadows drifted through his eyes like a stark Ansel Adams landscape playing out across Duarte's face. Then he smiled, cupping her head to draw her mouth to his.

The breeze blew over her again, chilling her through as she thought of how he'd opened up to her, and wondering if in her fear she'd fallen short in giving him her trust.

They'd eaten an honest-to-goodness family dinner.

Working his kinked neck from side to side, Duarte cradled his post-meal brandy in the music room. Well, it was more of a ballroom actually, with wooden floors stretching across and a coffered ceiling that added texture as well as sound control. Crystal chandeliers and sconces glowed.

And the gang was all here, except for Carlos, of course. But their numbers had grown all the same.

Shannon played the piano, her son seated beside her

with his feet swinging. Tony leaned against the Steinway Grand, eyes locked on his fiancée. His brother was one hundred percent a goner.

Sweet Jennifer sat cross-legged on the floor by the mammoth gold harp, petting Benito and Diablo, blessedly oblivious that she played with trained guard dogs while armed security flanked the door. What the hell had he brought Kate and her sister into?

Enrique reclined in a tapestry wingback chair, his feet on an ottoman. The bottle of oxygen tucked by a stained glass window reminded Duarte how very ill their father still was. Kate sat in the chair beside him, her foot tapping in time with the "Ragtime Waltz" that Shannon whipped through on the ivory keyboard.

Kate.

His eyes lingered on her. Her basic little black dress looked anything but basic on her curves he knew so intimately well. His gaze skated down her legs to her sky-high heels. If only they could stay in bed, this attempt at a relationship would be a piece of cake.

It had been tougher than he'd expected spilling his guts for her last night in the hammock, but that's what women wanted. Right? Yet somehow he'd missed the mark because still she held something back.

The last ragtime note faded, and Duarte joined in the applause.

Tony retrieved his drink from beside the music. "Hey, Kate, maybe you can persuade Duarte to play for us."

She turned toward him, surprise stamped on her face. "You play the piano?"

"Not well." Duarte lifted his drink in mocking toast to his brother. "Thanks, Tony. I won't be forgetting that. Keep it up and I'll tell them about your harp lessons."

Laughing lightly, Tony returned the air toast. Carlos

was the only one of them to catch on during music class. Tony had never been able to sit still long enough to practice. The teacher had told Duarte he played like a robot.

Great. Tally another vote for his inability to make an emotional commitment—even to a piece of music.

Enrique angled toward Kate. "Duarte might not have been the best musician, but my goal was simply to give my sons a taste of the arts so they received a well-rounded education. We may have been isolated, but I made sure they had top-notch tutors."

"Hmm." Kate nodded. "I don't see you as the sort of person who sits back and turns over control. So tell me, what did you teach them?"

"You are a good reporter."

"That's gracious of you to say." She winked at Enrique, as at ease with him as if she spoke with the mailman. "Considering who I work for."

"I taught my sons art history." Enrique continued on about his favorite Spanish masters.

Duarte swirled brandy in the snifter. Kate's jab at the *Intruder* surprised him. But then he'd seen her scruples show in the photos she chose. Would she have taken a job she didn't like just for Jennifer?

Of course she would.

His determination to win her over multiplied. He still had ten days left. His mind churned with plans to romance her between now and the wedding. Time to fly her to the Museum of Contemporary Photography in Chicago, to live out the pretend courtship they'd concocted.

She might not have understood that he was reaching out last night. But he could tap every last resource in the coming days up to the wedding to ensure she stayed.

His will strengthened, Duarte looked forward to his first step—a surprise trip this weekend to woo her with art in the museum she'd never visited. He savored the vision of another plane ride with her until—

Tony waved for everyone's attention. He hefted Kolby up and slid his other arm around Shannon's waist. "We have an announcement to make. Since our family is here, why not proceed with the wedding? Or rather we will as soon as Carlos arrives in the morning."

Enrique's pocket watch slipped from his hand. Duarte lunged and scooped it up just shy of the floor.

"We don't want to wait until the end of the month," Tony said, his eyes zipping to their father just long enough for Duarte to catch his fear that any delay could be too late for Enrique. "We want to get married this weekend."

Duarte's brandy turned bitter in his mouth. They'd moved the wedding up, cutting short everything he needed to do to ensure Kate remained his forever. He only had her promise of cooperation until Tony and Shannon tied the knot. And after the wedding, Kate would have no reason to stay.

She'd asked for a day at a time. And his time with Kate had just been cut abruptly short.

Twelve

"You may kiss your bride," declared the priest, vestments draping from his arms as he blessed the newlyweds at the chapel's altar.

Kate blinked back tears, raised her camera and *click, clicked.* She'd photographed weddings to earn extra money in college, but she'd never witnessed a more emotional, heartfelt union. Tony and Shannon had exchanged their vows in a white stone church with a mission bell over the front doors. Duarte had told her the quaint chapel was the only thing on the island built to resemble a part of their old life. It wasn't large, but big enough to accommodate everyone here—Enrique, the rest of the Medina family, the island staff. Kate realized she and Jennifer were the only outsiders. Shannon had no family or friends attending other than her son, and Kate felt a kinship with the woman who'd faced the world alone.

Until now.

Once the embracing couple finished their kiss, they faced the select crowd, their happiness glowing as tangibly as the candlelight from their nighttime service. As Beethoven's "Ode to Joy" swelled from the pipe organ, Tony swept up the little ring bearer. Kolby hooked his arms around his new father's neck with complete trust and the happy family started down the aisle, wedding party trailing them.

The Medina princess Eloisa served as maid of honor in an emerald empire-waist gown. Her bouquet of evergreens and pink tropical flowers from the island was clasped over the barely visible bump of her newly announced pregnancy. As she passed her husband seated by the king on the front pew, she smiled with unabashed love.

Duarte followed, leanly intense and breathtakingly handsome in his tuxedo. She never in a million years would have sought out a mega-rich prince, yet the more she learned about Duarte the man, the more she wanted to be with him. To hell with day-by-day. She wanted to extend this beyond their deadline. She wanted to take that risk.

And then Duarte moved past her, followed by Carlos—the brother she hadn't met yet—ending the bridal party. Kate lowered her Canon. Carlos's steps were painstakingly slow as he limped down the aisle. He clearly could have used a cane. Something about the proud tilt of his chin told her that he'd opted to stand up for his brother on his own steam.

This wounded family was breaking her heart.

She brought her camera back to her face and kept it there all the way outside into the moonlit night. A flamenco guitarist played beneath the palm trees strung with tiny white lights.

Sweeping the crowd with her lens, she snapped photos randomly for the album she planned to give to Tony and Shannon. She would upload the images and burn a disc for the couple, presenting her gift at the reception in case she didn't see the newlyweds again.

Although maybe, just maybe… A wary thread of hope, of excitement whispered through her.

She adjusted her focus on Jennifer, her sister's face animated as she took in the lights twinkling overhead in the trees. Love for her sister filled her. Jennifer wasn't a burden, but protecting her innocence was a responsibility Kate didn't take lightly.

A wide smile creased Jennifer's cheeks and she waved enthusiastically until Duarte stepped into the picture.

"Yes, Jennifer?" His voice carried on the ocean wind. "What can I do for you?"

"I don't need anything," Jennifer answered. "You do lots for everybody. I wanted to do something for you."

Jennifer extended her fist. Duarte's face creased with confusion.

"This is for you," Jennifer continued, dropping into his hand a beaded string of braided gold thread with a metal ring at one end, "since you're going to be my brother soon. I didn't think you would like a bracelet or a necklace like I make for Katie. But you drive a car, so I made you a key chain. Kolby's nanny got me the supplies. Do you like it?"

He held it up, ring dangling from his finger as he made a big show of admiring it. "It's very nice, Jennifer. Thank you. I will think of you whenever I use it."

"You're welcome, Artie—uh, I mean—"

"You can call me Artie," he said solemnly. "But only you. Okay?"

"Okay." Her smile lit her eyes as she rose up on her toes to give him a quick peck on the cheek before she raced across the sand toward the bridal party.

More than a little choked up, Kate swung the lens back to Duarte just as he pulled his keys from his pocket. Her breath hitched in her chest… He couldn't actually be planning to actually use it…

But, oh, my God, he attached the beaded gold braid alongside keys to his high-end cars and an island mansion. Thoughts winged back to that first night in Martha's Vineyard when they'd made up their mythical first date, complete with a vintage Jaguar and *cat*viar.

Her hands fell to her side, camera dangling from her clenched fist. Tears burned her eyes as she fell totally, irrevocably in love with Duarte Medina.

And she couldn't wait to tell him once they were alone together tonight.

The rest of the evening passed in a blur of happiness until before she knew it, Kate was waving to the departing newlyweds. Everything had been magical from the wedding to the reception in the ballroom with a harpist. She had almost hated to miss even a second when she'd slipped away to her computer to burn the disc. But she'd been rewarded for the effort when she pressed the DVD into Shannon's hand. They'd insisted they didn't want gifts, but every bride deserved a wedding album.

Kate arched on her toes to whisper in Duarte's ear. "I'm going upstairs to change. Join me soon? I have a special night planned that involves you, me and a tub full of bubbles."

"I'll be there before the bath fills."

The glint in his eyes spurred her to finish up her last bit of business all the faster.

In her room, she sat in front of the computer to dispense with this last obligation to Harold. Duarte had even given her the thumbs-up to select the wedding photos on her own. He trusted her...

Her computer fired up to the homepage and she logged on to the internet, eager to be done with this as quickly as possible so she could freshen up in a bubble bath and dig through the drawers of lingerie for just the right pieces. The news headlines popped onto the screen with thumbnail images. She frowned, looking closer in disbelief. Déjà vu hit her as she stared at the strangely familiar images.

Pictures of Tony and Shannon's wedding.

The same photos she'd loaded to make the disc, but hadn't yet sent to Harold.

Not just any photos, but *her* work all stored on this computer.

Confusion built as she clicked on article after article from different news outlets, all with photos she'd just taken tonight. How could this be? She flattened her hands to the computer that both Duarte and Javier had assured her only she and Duarte could access.

Had Javier turned on the family like his cousin? She quickly dismissed that possibility. Before she'd made that fateful trip to Martha's Vineyard, the *Intruder* had tried more than once to get the inside scoop from everyone in Duarte's employ. No luck there. Javier had stayed loyal. Which only left Duarte, and he'd made it clear from the start that he sought revenge for what she'd done to his family with her photo exposé.

Her heart shattering, she felt like such a fool. Duarte had wanted retribution and he had succeeded. He'd maintained total control of how his family appeared in the press. And he'd ensured she didn't profit a dime off her efforts.

She'd been so close to admitting she'd fallen in love with him. But she would be damned before she let him know just how deeply he'd wounded her.

Five more minutes and Duarte would finally have Kate alone. He didn't hear the bath running, but then if all went according to schedule, he would have her on an airplane soon.

Tony and Shannon's early wedding hadn't left him much time to expedite his plans to take Kate to the Chicago museum. But he'd pulled it together. A jet was waiting, fueled up and ready to wing them away from here.

All he needed was her okay on plans for Jennifer— he'd learned his lesson well on not usurping Kate when it came to her sister. Hopefully, after tonight he would have a larger role in her life, one where they shared responsibilities. He was determined to make his pitch in Chicago, to persuade her that they should extend their relationship beyond tonight, beyond the island.

Looking through the open doors, he saw her still sitting at the desk in her room in front of her computer, not in the tub but every bit as alluring to him even with her clothes on. So many times they'd gone over her pictures together before she had sent them. She'd been careful about giving him a chance to veto photographs even though more often than not she nixed a picture first. He didn't even feel the need to look over her shoulder now.

He trusted her. What a novel feeling that almost had

him reeling on his feet. He turned away to gather his thoughts, bracing a hand on his four-poster bed.

Fast on the heels of one thought came another. He more than trusted her. He'd been mesmerized by the woman who'd stood toe-to-toe with him from the start. Someone he could envision by his side for life.

He'd known he wanted her with him long-term, but how had he missed the final piece of the puzzle? That he loved her.

The sense of being watched crawled up his spine and he turned around to find Kate standing in his open doorway. And she didn't look happy.

Pale, she stood barefoot, still wearing the midnight-blue dress with Medina sapphires and diamonds.

He straightened, alarms clanging in his brain. "What's wrong?"

Blinking back the shine of tears and disbelief in her eyes, she braced herself against the door frame. "You sold me out. You released my photos of the wedding to the press."

What the hell? He started toward her, then stopped short at the fury in her eyes. "Kate, I have no idea what you're talking about."

"Is that how you want to play this? Fine, then." She dropped her hands from the doorway, her fists shaking at her side. "I started to send the wedding photos, only to find they had already been released to every other media outlet. My big scoop stolen from me." She snapped her fingers. "That fast. You're the one who gave me that computer, totally secure you assured me. You were very specific about the fact that only you and I had access. What else am I supposed to think? If there's another explanation, please tell me."

Every word from her mouth pierced through him

like bullets, riddling him with disillusionment, pain, and hell, yes, anger. He may have decided he trusted her, but clearly that feeling wasn't returned.

"You seem to have everything figured out."

"You're not even going to deny it? You've had this planned from the start, your revenge on me for the story I broke exposing your family." Her composure brittle, she still stood her ground. "I was such a fool to trust you, to let myself care—"

Her throat moved with a long swallow as his plans crumbled around him. She'd clearly made up her mind about him. It was one thing if she had concerns or reservations, but for her to blatantly question his honor. She could ask for explanations all night long. Pride kept his mouth sealed shut.

Face tipped, she met his gaze without flinching. "I knew you were ruthless, but I never even saw this coming."

Was that a hint of hurt, a glint of regret in her watery blue eyes? If so, she had a damned strange way of showing it.

"You climbed onto my balcony to steal a picture." He tapped one of her earrings quickly before she could back away. "Sounds like we're a perfect, ruthless match."

She pulled off both earrings and slapped them into his palm. Her chin quivered for the first time and fool that he was, he couldn't bring himself to wound her further.

He pivoted away, hard and fast, earrings cutting into his fist. "There's a plane fueled up and ready on the runway. I'll send instructions to the pilot to take you and Jennifer back to Boston."

Watching her reflection in the mirror, he caught his last glimpse of Kate as she slipped the ruby engagement ring from her finger, placed it on his dresser and walked out of his life as barefoot as she'd entered.

Strapped into the private plane, Kate stared out the window at the fading view of the island lights. The shades would come down soon and the magical place would vanish like some Spanish Brigadoon.

Within an hour of her fight with Duarte, she and Jennifer were airborne as he'd promised. How could she have been so completely duped by him? From the second she'd found the internet explosion, she'd hoped he would explain how wrong she'd been. Even with the evidence barking that he'd set her up from the start, Kate had hoped he would reassure her of his love and come up with an explanation for the mysteriously leaked photos...

She didn't pretend to understand him. But then, he'd refused to explain himself, refused to give her even the satisfaction of knowing why he would choose this means for his revenge.

Jennifer sniffled beside her, a Kleenex wadded in her hand. "Why can't we stay at the island?"

Most of all, she hated the hurt she'd brought to her sister. How could plans to provide a better life for Jennifer have gone so wrong? "I have to work, honey. How about you just try to get some sleep. It's been an exhausting day."

They'd come a long way from the excitement of preparing for the wedding. She'd had such high hopes a few short hours ago.

"Why did you break up? If you're married to Duarte, you won't have to work anymore." She tore the wadded tissue then clumped it together again.

"It isn't that simple." Nothing about her time with Duarte had been simple.

"Then why did you get engaged?"

As hurt and angry as she felt, she couldn't put the entire blame on Duarte. She'd played her own part, going in with eyes wide-open, deceiving her sister and so many other good people. She deserved all the guilt Jennifer threw her way. "People change their minds, and it's good if that can happen before the couple walks down the aisle."

"But you love him, right?"

Unshed tears burned her eyes, tears that had been building since she'd stared at that computer. She didn't understand why he'd given her the Ansel Adams. Why he'd indulged her sister in a private moment with the key chain, never knowing Kate had been watching the whole time. Kate couldn't explain any of the moments he'd been so thoughtful and warm, appearing to share a piece of himself with her. But she understood the missing photographs hadn't sent themselves.

Her heart hurt so damn much.

Her sister thrust a fresh Kleenex into her hands. "Katie, I'm sorry. I didn't mean it." Jennifer hugged her hard. "You shouldn't marry him for me. You should only marry him if he loves you, like in Cinderella and Beauty and the Beast, except Duarte's not a beast. He just scowls a lot. But I think it's because he's unhappy."

"Jennifer." Kate eased back, clasping her sister's hand and searching for the right words to make her understand without hurting her more. "He doesn't love me. Okay? It's that simple, and I'm really sorry you got so attached to all the pampering and the people."

Most of all, the people.

"You're my family." Jennifer squeezed their clasped

hands. "We stick together. I don't need any spa stuff. I can paint my own fingernails."

The hovering tears welled over and down her cheeks. She didn't deserve such a dear sister. "We'll go shopping together for different colors."

"Blue," Jennifer said, her smile wide, her eyes concerned, "I want blue fingernails."

"It's a deal."

Jennifer hugged her a fast final time and reclined back in her seat, asleep before the steward came through to close the window shades. With a simple request for blue nail polish, Jennifer had given Kate a refresher course on the important things in life. Like her values. If she expected to be a true role model for her sister, she needed to reorganize her priorities. Jennifer deserved a better sister than someone who crept around on ledges to steal a private moment from someone's life.

Even if it meant hanging up her camera for good.

Thirteen

"Didn't you forget something?" Enrique asked from his bed.

His father's question stopped Duarte in his tracks halfway to the door. "And what would that be?" He pivoted toward Enrique, the old king perched on his comforter with his breakfast tray. "You asked me to bring your morning coffee and churros from the kitchen. If something's wrong you'll need to take that up with the chef."

"You forgot to bring your fiancée."

Was Enrique losing his memory? Duarte had already told him about the broken engagement when he'd asked for the tray in the first place. Concern for his dad's health momentarily pushed Duarte's mood aside. "She and I broke things off. I told you already. Don't you remember?"

His father pointed a sterling silver coffee spoon at

him. "I remember perfectly well the load of bull you fed me about going your separate ways. I think you screwed up, and you let her go."

He hadn't *let* her go. Kate had walked out on him, more like *stormed* away, actually. And even though he had a pretty good idea who'd stolen her photos and sold them to other outlets, that didn't change the way she'd believed the worst of him.

Not that he intended to let the individual who'd broken into her computer and taken her work get away with it. Since she had only used the computer for work while on the island, he would bet money her editor had had his IT department hack her account during communications about prior photos. Then Harold Hough had probably sold the pictures to other outlets for personal profit. The Medina computers had top-notch security, but no cyber system was completely immune to attack.

By the end of today, Javier and his team would hopefully have proof. Then Duarte would quietly make sure Harold Hough never took advantage of Kate again. While that wouldn't heal the hole in his heart over losing her, he couldn't ignore the need to protect her. More than his own hurt at losing her, he felt her losses so damn much. He hated the idea that she'd lost her big payday and was right back in a difficult situation with her sister's care.

"Well?" his father pressed.

Duarte dropped into a chair beside his father's bed with four posters as large as tree trunks. "Sorry to disappoint you." Best to come clean with the whole mess so his father wouldn't keep pestering him to chase after Kate. "We were never really engaged in the first place."

"And you think I didn't know that?" His father eyed him over the rim of his bone china coffee cup.

"Then why did you let me bring her here?" Maybe he could have been saved the stabbing pain over losing Kate.

Except that would have meant giving up these past weeks with her, and he couldn't bring himself to wish away their time together.

Enrique replaced his cup on the carved teak tray. "I was curious about the woman who enticed you to play such an elaborate charade."

"Has your curiosity been satisfied?"

"Does it matter?" His father broke a cakey churros stick in half and dipped it in his coffee. "You've disappointed me by letting her leave."

"I'm not five years old. I do not need your approval." And he did not have to sit here and take this off his dad just because Enrique was sick. Duarte gripped the arms of the chair and started to rise.

"Since you are grieving, I will forgive your rudeness. I understand the pain of losing a loved one."

Duarte reeled from his father's direct jab. He'd had enough of the old man's games. If he wanted a reconciliation, this was a weird way to go about it. "Strange thing about *my* grief, I don't feel the least bit compelled to jump in bed with another woman right now."

Flinching, Enrique nodded curtly. "Fair enough. I will give you that shot." Then his eyes narrowed with a sharpness that no illness could dull. "Interesting though that you do not deny loving Kate Harper."

Denying it wouldn't serve any purpose. "She has made her choice. She believes I betrayed her and there's no convincing her otherwise."

"It does not appear to me that you tried very hard to change her mind." Enrique fished in the pocket of his robe and pulled out his watch, chain jingling. "Pride can cost a man too much. I did not believe my advisers who told me my government would be overthrown, that I should take my family and leave. I was too proud. I considered myself, my rule, invincible and I waited too long."

Enrique's thumb swept over the glass faceplate on the antique timepiece, his eyes taking on a faraway look the deeper he waded into the past. "Your mother paid the price for my hubris. I may not have grieved for her in a manner that meets your approval, but never doubt for a minute that I loved her deeply."

His father's gaze cleared and he looked at Duarte, giving his son a rare peek inside the man he'd been, how much he'd lost.

"*Mi hijo,* my son," his father continued, "I have spent a lot of years replaying those days in my mind, thinking how I could have done things differently. It is easy to torment yourself with how life could be by changing just one moment." Gold chain between two fingers, he dangled the pocket watch. "But over time, I've come to realize our lives cannot be condensed into a single second. Rather we are the sum of all the choices we make along the way."

The Dali slippery-watch artwork spoke to him from the walls in a way he'd never imagined. Lost time had haunted his father more than Duarte had ever guessed. During all those art lessons his father had overseen, Enrique had been trying to share things about himself he'd been too wounded to put into words.

"Your Kate made a mistake in believing you would betray her. Are *you* going to let your whole life boil down to this moment where you make the mistake of letting your pride keep you from going after her?"

He'd always considered himself a man of action, yet he'd stumbled here when it counted most with Kate. Whether he'd held back out of pride or some holdover pain from losing his mother, he didn't know. But as he stared at the second hand *tick, tick, ticking* away on his watch, he *did* know he couldn't let Kate slip out of his life without a fight.

And now that he'd jump-started his mind out of limbo, he knew just the way to take care of Harold Hough and let Kate know how much faith he had in her. But first, he had barely enough time to extend his father an olive branch that was long overdue.

"Thank you, *mi padre*." He clenched the old man's hand, grateful for the gift of a second chance.

January winds bitterly cold in Boston, Kate anchored her scarf, picking her way down the snowy sidewalk— toward the redbrick building that housed the *Global Intruder*. Not an overly large place, the *Intruder* head- quarters conducted most of its business online. She'd dreamed of a more auspicious retirement when the time came to hang up her media credentials.

But she didn't doubt her decision for a minute.

If she spent the rest of her life taking family portraits for tourists, then so be it. She had found a day facility for Jennifer, but her sister would be living with her. Hesitating at the front steps, Kate rubbed the braided charm that now hung on her camera case, the anklet she'd worn for luck not so long ago.

At least she would have her integrity, if not Duarte. She squeezed her eyes closed against the dull throbbing pain that hadn't eased one bit in spite of two nights spent soaking her pillow with tears.

A well-tuned car hummed in the distance, louder as it neared. She hopped farther onto the sidewalk to avoid a possible wave of sludge. How long had she stood on the curb of the one-way street?

She glanced over her shoulder just as a vintage Jaguar with tinted windows pulled alongside her. Her heart kicked up a notch as she wondered could it possibly be... A *red* vintage Jaguar, like the one Duarte had told her that he owned when they planned out their faux first date.

The driver's side door swept open and Duarte stepped out into the swirl of snowflakes. Long-legged, lean and every bit as darkly handsome as she remembered, he studied her over the roof of the car. She couldn't see his eyes behind the sunglasses, but his shoulders were braced with a determination she recognized well.

While she didn't know how to reconcile her heart to what he'd done with the photos, she couldn't stifle the joy she felt over seeing him here. Without question, he'd come for her. She hoped her weak knees would man-up before she did something crazy like walk right back into his arms.

Securing her camera bag on her shoulder, she walked closer to the car, appreciating the barrier between them. "Why are you here?"

"Because this is where you are. Jennifer told me."

"Not for much longer." She clutched her bag, too weary to give him a hard time for calling her sister. Jennifer missed "Artie" no matter what a brave face she put on. "I'm quitting my job at the *Intruder.*"

"Why don't you hold off on that for a few minutes and take a ride with me first?" He peered over his sunglasses.

"You may not have noticed, but we're starting to attract a crowd."

Jolting, she looked around. Cars were slowing with rubberneckers, pedestrians who would normally hurry to get in out of the cold were staring curiously at the man who looked just like...

Heaven help her, they were celebrities.

Kate yanked open the passenger-side door. "Let's go."

Leaping into the low-slung vehicle, she clicked the seat belt into place, securing her into the pristinely restored Jag just as he slid the car into drive.

And didn't Duarte have a way of dragging her into his world when she least expected it? Sweeping snow from her coat, she cursed her weak knees, but she couldn't regret ditching the gathering throng. Funny how a red Jag drew attention. A Medina man beside it didn't hurt, either.

He dropped a large envelope onto her lap.

"What's this?" She thumbed the edge of what appeared to be a stack of papers.

"Documents transferring ownership of the *Global Intruder* to you."

Shock sparked through her, as blinding as the morning sun through the windshield.

"I don't understand." And she couldn't accept it if he offered it out of some sense of guilt over what he'd done to her. She thrust the papers back toward him. "No, thank you. I can't be bought."

Not anymore.

"That's not my intent at all." He guided the sports car effortlessly over the ice along narrow historic roads. "You lost out on the payment for your end of the bargain for the wedding photos. You even left behind the other pictures you took that the public hasn't seen. Why did you do that?"

"Why did you buy the *Intruder* for me?"

"You have a voice and honor I respect," he answered without hesitation. "I know you'll bring humanity to the stories you cover."

"You want me to work for you?"

"You're not listening." Pausing at a stoplight, he turned to face her and pulled off his sunglasses. Dark shadows of sleeplessness marked beneath his eyes much like the weariness on her face. "The *Intruder* is yours regardless. But it is my hope that you'll accept my apology for not clearing the air the minute you came into my room after the wedding."

The magnetism of his deep onyx eyes drew her even when she guarded her heart. Much longer alone with him and she would cave to the wary hope spiraling through her like smoke from the chimneys.

"All right." She hugged the papers to her chest like a protective shield, wondering how Duarte had managed this all so fast. But then he was a man of decisive action when he chose to be. "I accept the apology and the *Intruder*. You're off the hook. You can leave with a clear conscience."

He parked on the roadside within sight of Long Wharf and the Aquarium, the tinted windows shielding them from view.

Turning toward her, he pulled off his gloves and cupped her shoulders in a gentle grip. "I don't want to leave. I want you. And not just today, but forever if you'll have me."

Just like that, he thought he could drive up and buy her off with a big—albeit amazing—gift? She looked away from his magnetic eyes. Think, she needed to think.

She stared at his key chain swaying in the ignition. She struggled to be reasonable, for Jennifer's sake. Her sister had been so crushed over the breakup, Kate needed to be completely certain before she invited Duarte back into her life. Jennifer had braided that key chain for Duarte with such hope and love...

She tapped the swaying braid attached to Duarte's keys. "You kept Jennifer's present."

Frowning, he hooked his arm on the steering wheel. "Of course I did. What of it?"

The way he hadn't even considered hiding or tossing aside Jennifer's gift opened Kate's eyes in a way nothing else had. Like someone had taken off the lens cap, she saw him, really saw him for the first time. And in that flash she saw so many things clearly.

"*You* didn't distribute my photos," she said, her voice soft. "You didn't try to lash out at me for revenge."

He stroked back her hair with lingering, delicious attention to her sensitive earlobe. "I did not betray you, but I understand how it could be difficult for you to trust me."

What she'd realized—after seeing the key chain, hearing him say the words, witnessing the honesty in his eyes—felt so damn good. The love she'd only just found took root and began to flourish again. "Thank you for being the calm, reasonable one here. I don't even know how to begin to apologize for assuming the worst of you."

What it must have taken for a proud man like Duarte to overlook her accusation and come for her anyway. Regret burned right alongside the joy until she promised herself to make it up to him.

"Kate, I realize your father hasn't given you much reason to have faith in men or trust a man will be there for you." His palm sought the small of her back, drawing her closer. "I want the chance, I want the *time* to help you put that behind you. Most of all, I just want *you*."

Gripping the lapels of his wool coat, she brushed her lips over his. "I have one question for you."

The hard muscles along his chest tensed, bracing. "Okay, I'm ready."

"Can we spend a lot of that time making love?"

"Absolutely." He slanted his mouth over hers, familiar, stirring, a man confident in the knowledge of exactly what turned his lover inside out.

Five breathless heartbeats later, Kate rested her forehead against his. "I can't believe you bought the *Intruder*."

"I had to figure out a way to fire Harold Hough."

"You fired Harold?" Thinking of her boss's threat to expose Jennifer to the harsh light of the media, Kate didn't bother holding back the downright glee at hearing he'd gotten his just deserts.

"Inside that envelope you'll also see some of the proof Javier put together showing how Hough is responsible for selling all those photos to other media outlets. He pocketed the money for himself. He accessed your computer through a virus he sent in an email. After a, uh, discussion with me, he decided it was prudent to step aside and avoid a lawsuit."

"Why didn't you tell me this the second we got in the car together?"

"It was nice having you decide to trust me on your own. Although if you hadn't, I would have still pulled the plug on Harold for what he did to you and our family."

Our family.

He'd said it without hesitation, and she couldn't miss the significance.

"I want you to help me house hunt."

Now *that* declaration surprised her. He spoke like a man ready to put down roots, a man coming to peace with his past.

"You're really ready to give up the cushy hotel living?"

"I was thinking of something on the outskirts of Boston, large and on the water. Big enough for you to move in when you're ready, Jennifer, too." His accent thickened as it always did when emotion tugged at him.

"I love you, Kate. While I'm willing to give you all the time you need, I don't need more time to be sure of that."

He reached into his pocket and pulled out her ruby-and-diamond engagement ring. "This is yours now. Even if you walk away, no other woman will wear it. It will always be waiting for you."

The beauty of his words, his whole grand gesture in coming here and presenting her with the *Intruder,* offering to buy a house calmed any reservations. She peeled off her glove and offered her hand without a second thought. He slid the ring back in place and she knew this time, it would stay there.

Duarte closed his hand around hers and rested it over his heart. "Did you notice the car?"

"Your vintage Jaguar…" How far they'd come since that night she'd scaled the outside of his resort.

"I told you I would pick you up in it for our first date. Do you remember where we would go?"

"The Museum of Contemporary Photography in Chicago." How could she forget?

"And before you can protest, remember you own the *Intruder* so you can give yourself at least twenty-four hours off to regroup. If it's okay with you, I would like Jennifer to meet us at the plane. And lastly, you can bring your cat. It's my plane, after all. And—"

"No more details." She covered his mouth with her hand playfully. "Yes, I trust you completely with my life, my sister, my heart."

"Thank you." His eyes closed for a moment, the sigh shuddering through him telling her just how much her rejection had wounded him. She vowed to show him how dear he'd become to her in such a short time, and could only imagine how much more he would mean to her in the coming years.

His eyes opened again and he pressed a tender kiss into her palm. "So what about that trip to Chicago? Are you ready to leave?"

She slipped her arms around his neck and her heart into her eyes. "Yes, I will go to Chicago with you and house hunt after we return. I will wear your ring, be your princess, your wife, your friend for the next thirty days, thirty years and beyond."

Epilogue

Wind whipped in off the harbor, slapping the green bathrobe around Kate's legs. Her cold toes curled inside her slippers as she stood on the balcony of Duarte's Martha's Vineyard resort.

The lighthouse swooped a dim beam through the cottony-thick fog, Klaxon wailing every twenty seconds and temporarily drowning out the sounds from an early Valentine's party on the first floor.

A hand clamped around her wrist. A strong hand. A *masculine* hand.

Grinning, Kate turned slowly. His fingers seared her freezing skin just over her newest braided bracelet made by her sister. A good luck charm to celebrate her engagement. And Kate certainly hoped to get lucky in about five more minutes.

Nestled against the warm wall of her fiancé's chest, she savored the crisp chest hair, defined muscles and musky perspiration. Oh, yeah, she was more than a little turned on. Kate stared her fill at the broad male torso an inch from her nose. A black martial arts jacket hung open, exposing darkly tanned skin and brown hair. Her fingers clenched in the silky fabric of his ninja workout clothes.

Kate looked up the strong column of *her* ninja's neck, the tensed line of his square jaw in need of a shave, peering into the same coal-black eyes she'd photographed many times.

"You're not a ninja," she teased.

"And you are not much of an acrobat." Prince Duarte Medina didn't smile. But he winked.

The restrained strength of his calloused fingers sparked a welcomed shiver of awareness along her chilled skin.

"We should go back inside before you freeze out here."

"The moonlight on the water is just so beautiful." She leaned into the warmth of his chest, now plenty toasty thanks to the heat he generated with just a glance her way. "Let's stay for just another minute."

There hadn't been many seconds spent standing still over the past couple weeks. After returning from Chicago, they'd gone by the island to visit his father. Seated around the dinner table, Enrique had announced he intended to go to a mainland hospital for further assessment. A hospital in *Florida*.

If she'd put her mind to it, she probably could have guessed the Medina island was off the coast of St. Augustine, Florida, given the weather. And while the island sported a mix of English, Spanish and even a little French...her journalistic instincts said the place carried an American influence. But admitting that to herself then would have been more knowledge than she was comfortable having.

Knowledge that had far-reaching safety implications for the Medinas.

And now that she was a de facto Medina by engagement, she had a whole new perspective on the PR angle. No doubt, handling publicity for the Medina family would be a full-time job. She had retooled the *Global Intruder* into *Global Communications*.

Arching up, she kissed her fiancé, who also happened to be the proud new owner of a sprawling Boston mansion on the water, a forever home with room for Jennifer and any future little princes and princesses. "I love you, Duarte Medina."

"And I love you." He swept her up, sporting real strength to go with those ninja workout clothes. Strength and honor to count on for life.

* * * * *

*Look for Carlos's story,
coming soon from Silhouette Desire.*

Silhouette Desire

COMING NEXT MONTH
Available February 8, 2011

#2065 THE BILLIONAIRE GETS HIS WAY
Elizabeth Bevarly

#2066 SEDUCED: THE UNEXPECTED VIRGIN
Emily McKay
The Takeover

#2067 THE BOSS'S BABY AFFAIR
Tessa Radley
Billionaires and Babies

#2068 TAMING THE VIP PLAYBOY
Katherine Garbera
Miami Nights

#2069 TO TEMPT A SHEIKH
Olivia Gates
Pride of Zohayd

#2070 MILLION-DOLLAR AMNESIA SCANDAL
Rachel Bailey

REQUEST YOUR FREE B[

2 FREE NOVELS PLUS 2 FREE GIFTS!

Silhouette® Desire®

Passionate, Powerful, Provocative!

YES! Please send me 2 FREE Silhouette Desire® novels and my 2 FREE gifts (gifts are worth about $10). After receiving them, if I don't wish to receive any more books, I can return the shipping statement marked "cancel." If I don't cancel, I will receive 6 brand-new novels every month and be billed just $4.05 per book in the U.S. or $4.74 per book in Canada. That's a saving of at least 15% off the cover price! It's quite a bargain! Shipping and handling is just 50¢ per book.* I understand that accepting the 2 free books and gifts places me under no obligation to buy anything. I can always return a shipment and cancel at any time. Even if I never buy another book, the two free books and gifts are mine to keep forever.

225/326 SDN E5QG

Name _____ (PLEASE PRINT) _____

Address _____ Apt. # _____

City _____ State/Prov. _____ Zip/Postal Code _____

Signature (if under 18, a parent or guardian must sign)

Mail to the **Silhouette Reader Service**:

IN U.S.A.: P.O. Box 1867, Buffalo, NY 14240-1867
IN CANADA: P.O. Box 609, Fort Erie, Ontario L2A 5X3

Not valid for current subscribers to Silhouette Desire books.

Want to try two free books from another line?
Call 1-800-873-8635 or visit www.morefreebooks.com.

* Terms and prices subject to change without notice. Prices do not include applicable taxes. N.Y. residents add applicable sales tax. Canadian residents will be charged applicable provincial taxes and GST. Offer not valid in Quebec. This offer is limited to one order per household. All orders subject to approval. Credit or debit balances in a customer's account(s) may be offset by any other outstanding balance owed by or to the customer. Please allow 4 to 6 weeks for delivery. Offer available while quantities last.

Your Privacy: Silhouette Books is committed to protecting your privacy. Our Privacy Policy is available online at www.eHarlequin.com or upon request from the Reader Service. From time to time we make our lists of customers available to reputable third parties who may have a product or service of interest to you. If you would prefer we not share your name and address, please check here. ☐

Help us get it right—We strive for accurate, respectful and relevant communications. To clarify or modify your communication preferences, visit us at www.ReaderService.com/consumerschoice.

SDES10R

HARLEQUIN®

A Romance

FOR EVERY MOOD™

Spotlight on

Classic

Quintessential, modern love stories
that are romance at its finest.

See the next page
to enjoy a sneak peek from
the Harlequin® Romance series.

THE SQUAWKING QUIETED as Elli picked the baby up, and
Wyatt turned around, trying hard to ignore the feelings of
inadequacy as Darcy immediately stopped fussing.

"Maybe she's uncomfortable. What do you think, sweet-
heart?" Elli turned her conversation to the baby.

"What do you think is wrong?" Wyatt asked, putting the
coffee pot back on the burner.

A strange look passed over Elli's face, one that looked
like guilt and panic. But it was gone quickly. "I couldn't
say," she replied.

"But you were so good with her this afternoon." Wyatt
put his hands on his hips.

"Lucky, that's all. I just...remembered a few things."
The same strange look flitted over her features once more.

Wyatt took the coffee to the table. "You fooled me. You
looked like you knew exactly what you were doing." So
much so that Wyatt had felt completely inept. A feeling he
despised. He was used to being the one in control.

Elli and Darcy walked the length of the kitchen and
back. After a few moments, she admitted, "I haven't really
cared for a baby before. The things I thought of were simply
things I'd heard about. Not from experience, Mr. Black."

Her chin jutted up, closing the subject but making him

want to ask the questions now pulsing through his mind. But then he remembered the old saying—*Don't look a gift horse in the mouth.* He'd benefit from whatever insight she had and be glad of it.

"I don't really know what babies need," he said. "I fed her, patted her back like you did, walked her to sleep, but every time I put her down…"

Wyatt almost groaned. Of course. He'd forgotten one important thing. He'd been so focused on getting the formula the right temperature that he'd forgotten to check her diaper. Not that he had any clue what to do there either.

Pulling calves and shoveling out stalls was far less intimidating than one tiny newborn.

"She's probably due for a diaper change, isn't she." He tried to sound nonchalant. This was a perfect opportunity. Elli must know how to change a diaper. He could simply watch her so he'd know better for the next time.

Instead, Elli came around the corner of the counter and placed Darcy back in his arms. "Here you go, Uncle Wyatt," she said lightly. "You get diaper duty. I'll fix the coffee. Cream and sugar?"

Oh boy, Wyatt thought, looking down into Darcy's pursed face, his smug plan blown to smithereens. He was in for it now.

Will sparks fly between Elli and Wyatt?

Find out in
PROUD RANCHER, PRECIOUS BUNDLE
Available February 2011 from Harlequin Romance

Try these Healthy and Delicious Spring Rolls!

INGREDIENTS	DIRECTIONS
2 packages rice-paper spring roll wrappers (20 wrappers)	1. Soak one rice-paper wrapper in a large bowl of hot water until softened.
1 cup grated carrot	2. Place a pinch each of carrots, sprouts, cucumber, bell pepper and green onion on the wrapper toward the bottom third of the rice paper.
¼ cup bean sprouts	
1 cucumber, julienned	
1 red bell pepper, without stem and seeds, julienned	3. Fold ends in and roll tightly to enclose filling.
4 green onions finely chopped— use only the green part	4. Repeat with remaining wrappers. Chill before serving.

Find this and many more delectable recipes
including the perfect dipping sauce in